Peter Jordan has won various awards for his work, and has published over fifty short stories in literary magazines and journals. The first half of his adult life was spent drunk, but he got sober and began to write following a brain tumour. When he isn't writing short stories, he can still be found working as a journalist. He currently lives in Belfast with his wife, three children, dog, two cats, and bearded dragon.

Calls to
Distant Places

Peter Jordan

KINGSTON UNIVERSITY
PRESS

First published in 2019 by Kingston University Press.

A catalogue of this book is available from the British Library.

ISBN 978-1-909362-37-6

Typeset in Constantia
Cover image: Lee Phillips/Naqi Shahid

Edited by Cerian Fishlock, Beth Summers, Kelly Squires

Design and Production team: Lauren Tavella, Kelly Squires,
Beth Summers, Cerian Fishlock, Bianca Caministeanu

KINGSTON UNIVERSITY PRESS
Kingston University
Penrhyn Road
Kingston-upon-Thames
KT1 2EE

@PM_Jordan

There is a principle, which is a bar against all information, which is proof against all arguments, and which cannot fail to keep a man in everlasting ignorance – that principle is contempt prior to investigation.

– Herbert Spencer
Taken from *The Big Book*
Alcoholics Anonymous

For my mother, Patsy.
Thanks for everything Mum.

In magazines

I needed something I could sell. Something human.

Before lunch, a white Hilux pulled up at the British checkpoint. In the open back of the vehicle was a young man who'd been shot in the stomach.

He looked no older than sixteen, but he wore the steel-blue uniform of the Afghan Police.

I took a photograph.

Although in pain, he lifted his head and posed.

It was only later, when I looked closely at the shots, that I noticed he wore eyeliner.

The medic arrived and gave the boy a jab of morphine through the trouser leg of his uniform.

The driver of the Hilux, an older man in uniform, wanted to take the boy to the big American field hospital; but the medic told him the mountain road ahead was mined.

The driver looked along the road – like he was deciding on something – then he placed a cigarette in the boy's mouth.

I saw the medic slip the driver a syringe and vial. As he did so the boy asked a final question.

The interpreter looked to me and spoke softly.

– He'd like to know where the photographs will be shown.

I couldn't tell him they wouldn't be shown anywhere. It was the medic who spoke up.

– Tell him they'll be shown in the glossy American magazines.

When the interpreter relayed the message, the boy lit the cigarette and looked up at the endless blue sky.

For a long time I stood there in the dust watching the vehicle drive back up the slope, until it was no more than a speck on the high mountain.

Luna

She dragged him down through sixty feet of water to the deepest part of the pool. His ears popped on the way down. He remained calm. He loved this orca.

Her name was Luna.

She was the star attraction and the dominant female of the three orcas in the park. She was also the most emotionally intelligent animal – human or otherwise – he'd ever met.

He'd known her for twenty years. There were no other relationships in his life. No vacations. No sick days. There was nothing but Luna. It was his choice. The greatest choice he ever made.

Seated on the bottom, he pinched his nose and blew until the pressure in his ears equalized. From somewhere above he could hear the panicked whistles and shouts from the other trainers. They seemed so far away.

At the surface the two other orcas circled the pool at great speed, creating great waves. He could hear their excited vocalizations. Their high-pitched clicks and whistles. Their language.

Luna remained silent.

In the years of performing with her he'd learned to hold his breath for long periods. Held there on the very bottom, he looked at her massive form, and he remembered.

Everything changed the moment he met her. Instantly, he abandoned all future plans.

Back then he was an eighteen-year-old intern. She was four years old, already twelve feet in length, and weighing almost two tons.

He knew she'd been taken from Russian waters as an infant. To do that it was most likely her mother had been killed. Yet he'd trotted out the company line to tourists.

– All of our orcas have enriched lives. All are captive bred. They've never known the wild.

In the years that followed he felt the shame of his lies and, eventually, his silence. But what could he do... if he complained they'd replace him. The fear of losing her kept him quiet.

He was there for the birth of her daughter, Estrella.

Luna had encouraged the newborn to the surface for her first breath, nudging the baby upwards, knowing.

For five years the company had kept Estrella – hoping she would perform with her mother – until a decision was made, and the youngster was sold to a park in Europe.

When her daughter was taken, Luna had remained at the side of the pool for three days, spy-hopping, her head fully out of the water, nodding forward, her body vertical, making a vocalization he'd never heard before. It was long range. Anyone who heard it knew it was grief.

She changed after that in the way a person would change following the loss of a child. He felt it. He knew her like a man knows his long-term partner.

Seated there on the bottom of the pool, he looked into her eye. She refused to return his gaze. Instead, she released his ankle and nudged him back up through the water column.

At the surface he didn't call out. He sucked in air, stroked her massive head, kissed her, and remained calm.

The trainers shouted, blew whistles.

Luna released her grip.

Calmly, deliberately, he swam toward the edge of the pool.

Before he could get there, he felt her presence below him, her wake momentarily propelling him forward. Then he felt the grip of her mouth on his other ankle.

She took him down again, this time to the very place where her daughter had been born.

He was tiring now, almost at his limit.

He looked into her eye. She looked directly back. And he knew with certainty that this time she would hold him down for longer.

White goods

You sit forward on the edge of the sofa, waiting. The black Buddha ashtray you bought in Thailand sits at your feet.

There's a knock on the door. Another knock. You lean forward, stub out the cigarette in the ashtray, wipe the ash from your skirt, and get up slowly.

He says his name, but you don't catch it, he's here to clean the sofa. You booked it before the funeral.

– Sorry I'm late, he says. They sent me to another job.

– Will it take long?

– No, not long.

You watch him haul a heavy rectangular case into the living room, then go to his car for another, smaller case.

– Can I get you a tea or coffee?

– A cold drink would be nice.

You walk into the kitchen, go to the freezer for ice, but the freezer is empty. So, you run the tap a little longer until the water runs cold, then you fill the glass almost full. While carrying it to him – in the hallway – you take a sip, not knowing at all why.

– Ah cheers, he says, as you hand him the glass.

He drinks it all and wipes his mouth with the back of his hand.

– This is no ordinary cleaner, he says. It has twenty different uses.

He names about ten straight off then slows; occasionally saying another as he assembles it. Two shiny pipes are fitted together with a brush attachment for cleaning. Then he changes his mind, takes off one of the pipes before fitting everything to a black flexible tube that he screws onto a transparent cylinder.

– We ask customers to clear the area before we arrive. But most don't have time or forget.

– I'm sorry, you say. Things have been a little crazy recently.

You lift the ashtray, walk into the kitchen, pull out one of the two wooden chairs from under the kitchen table and sit down. The machine starts up in the living room. It's loud and there's a whirring sound, like there's something trapped inside desperately trying to get out.

You light another cigarette.

There's a photograph of Frank attached to the fridge with a magnet in the shape of a butterfly. The fridge freezer and washing machine are yours. Everything else belongs to the landlord.

You get up and look closely at the photograph. It was taken only a year ago at a party in the house. In the photograph he's happy, smiling and healthy; the life and soul. You think about that photograph; the cancer had probably already taken hold when you took that snap.

You slip the photograph from under the fridge magnet and place it in your purse.

This past summer you learned a new word: metastasise. At first you couldn't pronounce that word. Couldn't get your head around the second syllable. Then you learned to say it clearly, with authority, with fear. The cancer had started in his bowel, metastasised to his liver, his lungs, his brain, everywhere.

The final two weeks of his life were spent on that sofa. He never moved.

Near the end he had no gag reflex. You gave him the liquid ketamine – and the vodka – in a ten millilitre syringe, squeezing it gently into his mouth. He would thank you with his eyes, until; at the end he didn't even have the will to do that.

Since Frank's death you've hardly had time to think. Right now, you feel relief, relief for Frank, and for yourself. And you feel the blunt guilt of it.

In two days' time, you'll get the deposit back on the rent. Then you'll travel. You have no definite plan. Tomorrow you'll have to clear the house; get rid of all of Frank's possessions. His clothes, his records, his shoes, everything. After that there'll be nothing left of your life together. It will be as if you never were. You take another draw on the cigarette.

You look again at the fridge freezer.

When the cleaning guy comes back into the kitchen you're lost. He carries a little square piece of black velvet before him, carefully, like it's a small animal, places it on the table in front of you and unfolds each corner. In the middle of the velvet is a mound of dust.

– It's amazing what this machine collects, he says. Little bits of us really... skin, hair, it all adds up.

You look at the mound of dust.

– This may sound like a strange request. But I was wondering if you might let me keep this.

A difficult
low-light shot

I heard two shots. They were loud, and I knew they were close.

I looked out of the apartment window. Across the street, at the beginning of the next block, was the Superfresh. Shoppers, mostly women, were spilling out of the front of the store: screaming; panicked, running short distances, crouched low, looking for cover.

I hurried down the stairs, taking them two at a time and out of the front door.

A black kid was lying on his back on the sidewalk outside the Superfresh. I'd say he was somewhere between the ages of thirteen and fifteen, although he was at least as tall as me.

A woman was down on both knees bent over him, her head close to his, asking where he lived, where his mom was. I couldn't hear his answer. She was telling him he was going to be okay.

One leg was drawn up, and he was pressing down hard on the sole of his foot, like he was trying to push himself up the steep incline of the street. Below his sneakers, two little trails of blood met to form a pool. One came from a bullet to his groin, the other from a bullet to his chest.

He rolled onto his side, away from the woman, towards the brickwork. The back of his white T-shirt was red with blood. Then he curled into the fetal position and gasped for air, like he'd just surfaced from being underwater.

I'd never seen anything like it. I wanted to help; to make things right, but there was nothing I could do.

Some people came over to investigate, bent over, curious. The doors of the Superfresh opened as the people set off the sensors. Each time the doors swished open I got the smell of roast chicken, but it didn't make me hungry like it usually did.

Inside the store, a security guard was sitting on one of the wheeled checkout seats; his hat in one hand, a can of soda in the other. His partner was being given first aid on the polished floor.

First to arrive was Channel 10 News, a small cream-colored transit van with a satellite dish on top. A guy in a cream suit got out, followed by a cameraman. The cameraman hoisted the camera on to his shoulder as the man in the cream suit combed his hair.

I heard the ambulance before it arrived.

It parked up on the sidewalk; two paramedics got out and pulled their hands into tight blue plastic gloves. They both examined the boy. But he was dead.

The cops were the last to arrive. They got out of their patrol car with a tired but cautious look about them, in that slow way they do. Two big men, hats tipped back.

One cop was looking for witnesses, moving from person to person, wiping his face with a white hand-kerchief. The other cop walked into the Superfresh and talked to the security guards and staff. Those cops had seen it all before.

More patrol cars arrived, and these cops taped off the scene.

There was a semicircle of people now. Some local dudes sauntered over holding up the palms of their hands to stop the traffic. They wanted to know what had happened. There was a feeling in the air that things were over, but there was also a feeling that something else was yet to begin.

I walked back to the apartment block and closed the door behind me – stood for a minute in the coolness of the dim corridor – before walking up the flight of stairs to Cathal's apartment.

When I got inside, I locked the door.

The guy I shared the apartment with, Cathal, worked as a maintenance man in a nearby block of apartments. At night he was studying photography; he told me someday he'd work for *Playboy* magazine. He was good at what he did. On the walls of every room were photographs.

Only one of the photographs was framed – it was Cathal's all-time favorite – a close-up of a woman sitting on the front steps of a brownstone. Pulled tight over her scalp was a faded black bandana. Cathal said she'd just had a hit. Her pupils were blown, making her eyes look black, and she was smiling. When she smiled she hid her teeth. She could have been anywhere between the ages of seventeen and seventy.

The shot was in black and white. I remembered him telling me it was a difficult low-light shot.

That night, when Cathal arrived back from work I told him about the shooting.

He turned on the television and searched the channels until he found Channel 10 News. The guy in the cream suit with the combed hair was saying two young black kids had tried to rob two security guards. The two boys had used Tasers. One of the guards had been stunned and temporarily immobilized, but the other boy was slow, and the second security guard shot him twice.

Cathal kept pointing at the television and shouting: That's just next door. That's the fuckin' Superfresh.

When the news piece was over, Cathal got up and turned off the television. Then he lay down full stretch on the sofa, one leg drawn up, with his arms behind his head, and he said: Man, if only I'd seen that. That would've been some photograph.

I checked my watch. In an hour or so I'd take a shower, get ready to go out.

A picture of you

At the lakeside I stand on the jetty breaking bread, dropping it into the dark water, and I try to remember your face. But the face I remember isn't yours; the treatment has removed all of your hair, even your eyelashes have gone.

I stand like that and drift.

Then I glimpse a flash of gold in the water. A carp the size of a serving platter rolls on the surface.

I run up the grassy slope to our apartment and search for your toolbox.

Inside are your pliers with the worn yellow grips.

From the empty half of our bedroom wardrobe, I lift a wire coat hanger and snip off a short piece, twisting it at one end to form an eye. At the other end, I cut through the wire at an angle and curl the point into a hook.

Then I cut the string from the bedroom blinds and run back to the jetty.

But the carp has gone.

I lie there, the white string in the dark water, until

something yanks on my finger, something big. I haul it out onto the boards, but it isn't a carp, it's a catfish.

My hand under the soft white belly, I hold it gently.

From bitter experience, I know about those cruel spines. You took me fishing once and I lifted a catfish before you could warn me.

I remember the pain, and then I see your face – you're laughing – it's a picture of you the way I want to remember you, the way I need to remember you, and then you're gone.

And I think for a moment I might die. But, instead of dying, I remove the hook and let it go.

A tired person can sleep anywhere

The summer season was over, and the rest of the boardwalk was closed. Leo wondered why he opened the diner at all, when even the black-headed gulls that tormented the tourists had gone. He supposed, as much as anything, it was to give him something to do.

As he wiped the long Formica counter the door opened, and Maria hurried in.

– Man, it's dead out there, she said.

– You wanna start with a beer? asked Leo.

– Yeah, a cold beer sounds good.

Maria worked for the big hotel as a maid. Sometimes Leo would go back to Maria's and they would sit up and drink. One time they had both woken up in bed together, but nothing had happened. Leo was glad of that; he didn't want to ruin a good friendship.

He set up the beer.

– I'm starving, Leo, said Maria. What do you have

for me?

– Enchiladas sound good?

– Sounds perfect.

He served up the enchiladas.

– In the summer, the Hot Spot uses baked beans, said Maria. Can you believe that... baked beans!

– The tourists like it, said Leo.

– Tourists... what tourists?

They both laughed.

The door opened, and two men walked in. During the summer they worked as maintenance men on Morey's Pier; in the winter they were kept on as security, keeping the pier safe from drunken young-sters. They worked twelve-hour shifts, watched ball games, and smoked reefer. Every evening at six they came in, looked at the menu, and ordered cheese-burgers and fries. They would sit at the window with half an eye on the pier, smoking and drinking beer.

Both men took their usual seats at the window. The smaller of the two men placed two fingers up to Leo and Leo nodded.

He brought over two beers then he served up the cheeseburgers and fries. The smaller of the two men covered his fries in ketchup.

The door opened, and a young woman walked in.

The two men stopped eating.

She was beautiful. It was difficult to guess her age; Leo thought early twenties, she could be younger; it was hard to tell. She took a seat beside Maria at the counter.

Maria said: Hi, looked to Leo and said: Leo, meet Carla.

Leo wiped his hands on the front of his apron and shook her hand.

Without looking at the menu, Carla ordered pancakes. She ate only one, covered it in syrup – used up nearly half a bottle – but Leo didn't mind. After she finished eating, she lit up a cigarette.

– Filthy habit, said Leo, just by way of conversation; he smoked himself.

– There are worse habits.

– Yes, he said. There are.

He wanted to say more but found himself unable to think of anything appropriate. He hadn't felt this self-conscious since he was a teenager.

The girl got up, put a quarter in the jukebox, and selected a song Leo hadn't heard before. As the music played, she danced freely; head down, her arms across her chest, unaware of the men looking at her. When the song had finished, she ordered another beer, then went outside.

Leo looked over at the two men; they were both

looking at the closed door.

When she came back in and sat down, she was smiling. Then she dropped her chin to her chest and her dark brown hair hung over her face. When she raised her head, Leo could see her large brown eyes were glazed.

One of the security guards walked over. It wasn't the ketchup guy. It was the other one. Leo didn't like the man. He found him crude, sinister even.

– Can I buy you a beer?

She turned her head.

– Sure.

– Hey, said the guy. A Coors.

Leo set up the beer and moved away, but he was still within earshot. The guy came off with the usual lines. She was polite, patient, but in no way interested; after a time, he gave up and rejoined his friend at the window.

Maria and Carla drank on until closing, then each left with their shoes in one hand and their beer in the other.

Leo closed up, drank some beer and sat looking straight ahead. He thought this year would be his last. When he'd first taken over the business there was a T-shirt shop next door, now it was a 99 Cent store, next summer it would be something else. He'd have to take a hit on the lease but he could move back down to San Diego and stay with his mother until something else came along.

Every Christmas, when he closed the diner, Leo visited his mother. She was a good woman. He'd never known his father, hadn't even seen a photograph of him. His mother always told him he was like his father: constantly looking for something. Each time Leo arrived home his mother hugged him, then asked if he'd found what he was looking for. Leo would laugh it off, not letting his mother know how true it was, how deeply it hurt.

The next evening Leo stood behind the counter in a fresh apron. He served up the usual to the two security guys. They were the only people in the place.

When Maria came in, she noticed Leo's clean apron, the fact that he'd shaved. She ordered a beer then lit up a cigarette. Leo served up the beer and stood there in front of her.

– She started two days ago, said Maria. I don't know a lot about her.

Leo didn't say anything. He just listened.

– She can drink. I know that. When I woke up this morning she was gone.

– Where's she from? asked Leo.

Maria took a draw on the cigarette before

answering.

– She's from Tijuana.

Leo thought about that.

At six-thirty, Carla came in and sat down beside Maria. She smiled at Leo and ordered a beer. Then she got up, played the same song on the jukebox and danced in slow circles as she had the night before. The two security guys eyed her, exchanging remarks and laughing crudely. When the song finished, she went outside as she had the night before, only this time she didn't return.

– Hey, Maria, asked Leo. What the hell is that song?

– It's your jukebox, said Maria.

– It was here when I bought the place.

– You ever think of maybe getting something modern on it?

– The song Maria, what is it?

– Oh, I don't know... something about love and death.

The next day the two security guards came in.

– Hey, we saw your friend.

– She was asleep on the beach.

– Passed out, more like.

– In this weather, said Leo. Where'd you see her?

– Under Morey's Pier.

Leo set the men up two beers, took off his apron,

and threw it under the counter.

– Maria, he said. Keep an eye on things.

– Hey, said the taller one. What about my cheeseburger?

– You can wait, said Leo.

The wind blew sand along the boardwalk as Leo made his way down the wooden steps to the beach. He looked for the girl under Morey's Pier but there was no one there.

When he got back inside, he reached under the counter for his apron.

– Any sign? asked Maria.

– No, no sign.

– Any sign of that cheeseburger? said the ketchup guy.

– Hey buddy, fuck you… said Leo. You want something… go cook it yourself.

– Yeah, said the guy. Then I'll take my trade elsewhere.

– Yeah, you do that.

He got up and left. His friend stubbed out his cigarette, took a slow sip of his beer, and followed.

– Assholes, said Maria.

Leo cracked open a Coors.

– So, what's her story?

– I really don't know. Just passing through, I guess.

She looked out at the empty boardwalk.

– *A buen sueño no hay mala cama.*

– What does that mean? asked Leo.

– It's just a saying.

– What does it mean?

– It means a tired person can sleep anywhere.

The next afternoon Maria came in.

– Any news? asked Leo.

– You wanna let me get my coat off first?

Leo waited.

– She was owed two days wages, said Maria. She didn't even collect them.

– Then maybe something happened to her.

Maria looked away.

– Next summer I'm gonna move to the East Coast, she said.

– You say that every year.

– This time I mean it.

She took off her coat, draped it over the stool and sat down at the counter.

– At least the sun is out, she said.

– Beer?

– I'm gonna start with a coffee today.

Leo didn't speak over the noise of the espresso machine. He was tired; he hadn't slept well.

Maria drummed her fingers on the counter.

– You know what, she said. I will have that beer.

Leo went to the cooler, took out two Coors and removed the caps. He set one beer on the counter and took a quick drink from the other.

Maria raised the beer to her mouth, but she didn't drink from it.

– Leo, she said. Forget about her, she's gone.

Frogs

M y girl and I have made a pact to get clean.
As a final blowout we've booked into a chalet for two nights on someone else's credit card. The chalet is just five minutes' walk upriver from the main hotel. And the hotel is four-star.

The water is high when we arrive, and maybe a full sixty feet across to the far bank.

As my girl unpacks, I turn on the radio. For the remainder of the afternoon the radio plays in the background as we drink in the chalet.

Later that evening we get ready to go out; we've booked a table at the restaurant up at the main hotel.

I make an effort, and it's a long time since I've made an effort with anything. I don't shave, but I shower, and I dress in a clean white shirt, with clean trousers I wore once at a funeral. When I come out of the bathroom my girl is ready. She wears a black skater dress that runs to just above her knees.

– How do I look? she says.

– Beautiful, I say. You look beautiful.

She's lost some weight and there are bruises along the pale length of her legs, but she *is* beautiful.

It's just getting dark when we leave the chalet. We walk against the current, along the side of the slow water. In front of us, something jumps at our feet. I grab my girl, and she laughs.

– It's only a frog, she says.

It isn't a small frog. It's big. I don't like things like frogs. Before we met, my girl kept a pet lizard. In this way we're different; I don't even like dogs. I stand back and let the frog leap to the other side of the path and into the grass.

Hand in hand we walk the remainder of the distance up to the hotel for dinner. I'm creeped out by that frog. I up the pace and look behind me. My girl thinks this is hilarious.

The hotel is plush, expensive, but dressed as we are, we look like we belong. The waiter, a man in his sixties, is slow and precise in everything he does. And he's considerate; he pulls out a chair for my girl and she thanks him as she sits at the table. We don't order starters. The waiter recommends the sea bass. He calls me sir. I order it. My girl orders a vegetarian pasta dish.

Neither of us is as hungry as we thought. With our

meal, we have three bottles of white wine. When we get the bill the wine costs thirty quid a bottle. I have no cash to tip the waiter. I ask if he can put a fifteen per cent tip for himself on the credit card. He nods and wishes us a pleasant evening.

We sleep well that night and don't wake until the next afternoon. We talk about spending time in the health spa, it's free with the booking. My girl wants to try the swimming pool, maybe lie in the sauna. I want to try the Jacuzzi. But we don't go to the health spa; we get vodka and beer, and a single bottle of champagne, and we drink late into the evening.

– I can't take it anymore, says my girl. It's now beyond the point of fun.

– I agree... totally... that's why we're here on someone else's credit card.

While we talk there's a rap on the door.

I get up to answer it, but no one's there. I step outside, onto the wooden decking, but it's so dark and moonless I can't see a thing. Further along, upriver, I see some light reflected off the slack water, but there's definitely no one there.

– Who was it? she asks.

– The Grim Reaper.

– Don't say that. Please, don't say that now.

– It's no one... just the wind.

I sit down again and pour myself a large vodka and Coke.

As I sit sipping my drink, I hear two light thumps, one after the other.

My girl walks over, kisses me on the lips, and places her head on my shoulder.

– Is this real or is it just our messed up heads? she says.

– It's just the wind, that's all.

I sit for a while with my head on her chest listening to the slow pump from inside her ribcage, the blood flowing around her warm body.

She gets up off my knee and returns with the bottle of champagne, and I can see that she's crying.

I pop open the bottle and we toast our future, drinking from small white teacups.

She has brought H. That's her drug of choice.

After shooting up, she falls asleep. She always does this now, straight after.

I sit watching her sleep and I feel like the room's shrinking. This is to be my last drink, then a life forever without it, and I'm not sure if that's possible.

I get up and move around.

In my bare feet, I walk the length of the warm bedroom on the soft carpet to the cold tiles of the kitchen floor and back again to the patio door.

On the edge of the bed, I sit below my girl's bare feet. While I sit there, I hear that same thumping noise. It's hard to explain what it sounds like; it's not like someone knocking, it's much duller and flatter than that.

I turn my head sideways and call my girl's name, but she's asleep. Unsteadily, I get up, stand over her, move the hair from her face, and kiss her on the cheek.

I look again at her, and place two fingertips on her neck at the carotid artery. There's no pulse. She's cold. And I know that she's dead.

I lie down on the bed beside her, and for some reason none of this comes as a shock.

And then I hear that same thudding.

Slowly, I stand up, listening.

The noise is coming from the patio doors.

I slide them open but there's no one there. So I close the glass door tight, go back inside, get my mobile phone, and shine the torch. There are frogs throwing themselves at the bottom of the glass door. They do it like they're trying to pass through something. They've been doing this the whole time we sat talking. The whole time she lay dead.

Three days of rain

The house was a three-bedroom semi with a good-sized rear garden. I would live in the house, fit a new kitchen and bathroom, landscape the garden, and then put it on the market in the spring.

Fixing up houses is what I did. When I was fixing them up, doing the hard graft, I was fine. In between is where the problem lay; while waiting for a deal to finish I'd drink. That was the cycle.

My older brother was the first to suggest I had a problem; he guided me to Alcoholics Anonymous. He'd been sober for eleven years, did secretary at his home group, and helped a lot of people. I just wasn't ready for it.

The back garden of the new house was south facing and completely overgrown. So, I borrowed my brother's industrial strimmer. It took me a full four hours to cut the grass and weeds short enough just so I could mow it.

While I worked on that garden I felt good, there were no thoughts in my head.

To the right of the lawn was a raised section, built with flagstones, a perfect barbecue area. I planned on lifting the flagstones and replacing them with coloured cobbles. Little things like that help sell a house. And I was good at the little things.

At the very end of the garden, where it bordered the neighbour's, was a perfectly trimmed hedge. I looked over that hedge; the lawn next door was like a bowling green, cut in perfect lines. And, on either side of the back door of the house, were two large hanging baskets with flowering pink and red geraniums.

– Just moved in?

He caught me by surprise; he was bent down at the hedge, right in front of me, weeding.

– Jesus, you scared me...

He reached his hand over the hedge. It wasn't a tall hedge.

– Sorry, I didn't mean to scare you... my name's Norman.

– No... no problem. Pleased to meet you, I'm Jake.

I shook his hand over the hedge. I'd guess he was in his sixties. And he was slow and deliberate in his movements, his actions, his speech. He was everything I wasn't.

– Mrs Burke will be glad you're fixing up her garden, he said. She used to be in it every day.

Then he corrected himself.

– Well, I mean, it's your garden now.

– If I could get it like yours, I'd be happy.

He looked around at his own garden.

– Can I ask you a question?

– Fire away, he said.

– Those hanging baskets... how do you get them to flower like that?

– I'll let you into a secret, the deeper the basket the better the flower. You need to look after the roots. What's under the surface is the important part.

– I'll remember that the next time I hang one, I said. Thanks for the tip.

– No problem.

– I think I'll hang one at the back door. Just like yours.

He looked over the hedge to my back door, and he looked at the timber fences I had propped up there against the wall.

Then he angled his head slightly.

– Those fences, are they five feet?

– Yep, five feet, I said. I got them from Woodlands for a good price.

He placed his arms across his chest, his eyes narrowed.

– I hate to tell you this but... well, it's just the boundary fence can't be over four feet.

I didn't know what to say.

– Read the small print… really, he said. Your solicitor will confirm it.

I looked at the fences.

– Woodlands will replace them, he said. It's better you know now before putting them up.

I went inside, sat down at the kitchen table and lit a cigarette. But I couldn't settle. I walked from one room to another.

Then I went for a drink.

When I came home it was dark; I walked out into the back garden and pissed on Norman's hedge.

The next day, as soon as I woke, I started drinking again. I don't know how long it lasted… three, four days.

On the final morning someone was at the door, but I wasn't getting up for anyone.

Later that afternoon, I walked downstairs into the kitchen and made up some liver salts. Then I walked out into the garden and stood looking at the timber fences. Four feet… five feet… what the fuck did it matter? I didn't need to check the small print to know the neighbour was right. People like him were always right. I was shaking.

I walked back through the house, got in the car, and drove to the off-license.

When I got back to the house there was a hanging

basket on the front doorstep containing big red flowering geraniums. It was deep, with plenty of room for the roots. As soon as I saw that hanging basket I came right back to my senses.

I walked inside and put the bottle of vodka in the kitchen cupboard under the sink, behind the bleach and floor cleaner.

I knew I would need to be careful in the coming weeks: a credit card bill, an unexpected phone call, or three days of rain could set me off again. I went straight to bed, without anger, and slept right through to the next day.

The next morning, my brother was at the door.

– Where've you been? he said.

– Busy.

– Why didn't you answer yesterday?

– Yesterday?

– I came over... your car was in the driveway, but you didn't answer. Then I called back, and you were out.

– Oh... I said. Trouble with the neighbour, but don't worry, it's sorted.

He looked at me.

– I thought you were off it.

– I am off it.

He thought about that.

– Resentment is the number one offender, you

know that, don't you?

I wasn't in the mood for AA talk, or a lecture. I turned and walked to the kitchen.

My brother knew when to push me on something, and when to leave well alone.

I filled the kettle for coffee, then wondered if the milk was fresh.

– What do you think of the hanging basket? he said.

– It's good... plenty of room for the roots.

– I suppose...

Then he just stood there looking at me.

– So, are you going to thank me for it? he said.

– *You* brought the hanging basket?

– Yep, he said. Why, who did you think brought it?

All that water passing over the belly

It is late in the summer season and in a couple of hours it will be dark. At the entrance to the beach the litter bins are full to overflowing with plastic bottles, cans, and fast food wrappers. Sarah walks down from the warm tarmac to the beach with her surfboard under one arm and a canvas bag over her shoulder.

Waiting on the beach, Carlo looks out beyond the breakers to an area of flat water. In front of that flat water the belly of the sunken freighter is just visible. All that water passing over the belly makes for the perfect surf.

When Sarah joins him, they walk under the limestone cliffs.

All along the stretch of limestone are caves and arches.

At the entrance to a cave Sarah stops and sets the tail of the board in the soft white sand.

– It's like a church.

Carlo knows she's about to steer the conversation towards marriage.

– Here, he says. We'll leave the bags here.

He drops his bag on the dry sand and strides out with his board under one arm.

As the first wave crashes in, he jumps sideways on the tips of his toes, the board held high.

Between the next set of waves, he drops his board on the cold water and paddles out, steering between gaps in the oncoming swell. When he's far enough out he points the nose to shore, waiting for the right wave. Then he paddles furiously, catching the shoulder of it, and all in one movement he's upright, feeling for the grab and push and riding it all the way to the shallows.

The next wave, he mistimes, and is caught in the tumble dryer. Underwater, everything slows. He's no longer in control and, curled into the foetal position he feels the unfamiliar, thrilling fear of it.

For the next hour they surf.

Then Carlo paddles out the back, beyond the breakers to where the water is flat. For a short time he sits there watching her – his legs in the cold water — until the travelling clouds cover the sun and the water turns darker. At first there are just spits of rain, then as the main bulk of cloud rolls over, the rain pours from the sky in tight heavy drops.

The people on the beach scramble for cover: a mother with a toddler, two elderly women in long skirts with a little brown terrier. There are whoops and screams as the rain lashes down.

As quickly as it arrived it's gone. And suddenly the sun is out. It's as if it never happened.

Sarah paddles over to Carlo.

– Thank you, she says.

– For what?

– For this, she says, spreading her hands. All of this.

Carlo looks to the shore, to their bags.

– What's wrong? she asks.

– Nothing's wrong.

– No one's going to take anything, she says.

– I'm not worried about that.

– Then what are you worried about?

– Will we get out? he says.

– Ten more minutes.

– In ten minutes it'll be dark.

– You get out.

As Carlo paddles in he looks at the water in front. It's a blend of purple and green. He shivers and looks behind. Out to sea the water is black.

Where they laid their bags, the sand is soft and

dry. He sits down heavily and digs his heels roughly into the sand. It's warm on top, but cold just beneath the surface.

He looks out, just beyond Sarah to the sunken freighter, but the tide has risen, and nothing is showing.

When Sarah comes out of the water, Carlo is already dressed in jeans and a T-shirt.

She lays her board on the sand, kneels down, and kisses him.

– What's wrong? she asks.

– Nothing.

– Unzip me, then.

He pulls the blue cord at the back of her wetsuit.

– Reach me my top, will you, she says.

She dries herself, dresses quickly, and then sits on his towel beside him.

– Let's stay the night, she says.

– It's not a good idea.

– Why not?

– It's just not, that's all.

She places one arm across her stomach and looks directly at him.

– There's something I need to tell you, she says.

– Now is not a good time.

– Why... she asks again. What's wrong?

– Everything, he says, quickly.

– What do you mean, everything?

He doesn't answer.

Behind them is the vertical, white wall of limestone, in front of them the dark water.

Carlo, please tell me what's wrong?

He stares at his hands.

– I don't know what's wrong.

– Of course you know.

The waves are crawling further up the beach, leaving a wet, dark line in the sand. They are very close to this dark line.

– This isn't easy, he says. I don't know what to say.

– Then say nothing.

She gets up, hoists her canvas bag over her shoulder, bends at the knees, and lifts the board in the middle, under her arm.

He wants to say something, is about to, but realises there's nothing to say.

In a month it will all be sorted. He'll come out surfing on his own. The water will be colder by then, but he'll wear his winter wetsuit. He'll need his neoprene hood, gloves, and boots as well.

Between now and then there are things to be sorted. He'll play fair about it – the house is his, as regards everything else: half for her, half for him.

2020

Sergeant Grice stopped for a minute – the cold was shocking – his mind moved from ambush sites and firing zones to thoughts of home, his wife, his young son. This would be his last tour; everything had changed after his last visit home.

He looked across the slope to his men. Fungi carried an M4 assault rifle, which had been modified to fire big fat explosive 203s. Figgs carried the M24, a bolt-action sniper rifle with detachable scope, and their radio. Doc Zanetti, the medic, carried an M4 and was as dependable as anyone in a firefight.

They moved up, over a series of ridges and humps, sometimes crawling on their hands and knees when they came across the pockets of loose shale that were as sharp as flint. Each of them had become physically conditioned to Afghanistan: the high altitude, the stomach cramps; the searing heat, and the terrible cold. They were Olympic athletes who smoked sixty cigarettes a day. Their sweat reeked of ammonia; they'd lost all body fat, whatever they were burning now was muscle.

Over every hump Grice believed he would see a summit. Eventually, they came across some flat ground of coarse mountain grass that led, in turn, to a cliff. Built on the side of the cliff were cave houses, one wooden structure built on top of another, with a series of ladders and wooden walkways to each entrance. Grice stopped his men and scanned each entrance with his high-powered binoculars.

– Is this it? asked Doc.

– No. He lowered the binoculars. It's not on the map.

The men scanned the village through their riflescopes.

– Anyone see anything?

– It's abandoned, said Fungi.

– I think so, said Doc.

When the men were sure the village was safe, they chose a cave house large enough for the four of them. It had once housed a family and was surprisingly clean, sheltered, and comfortable. There was a main living room and two bedrooms.

From the front of the cave Grice had a perfect view. He looked straight up at the endless blue sky. On his last trip home he'd painted the ceiling of his son's nursery the same color of blue. And he'd added stars. He'd always hated painting, couldn't understand how anyone had the patience for it, but he'd enjoyed painting that nursery. He'd taken his time and, while doing it, his mind had settled completely. The painting of the stars was done with a child's paintbrush and some white gloss. He'd drawn each star first in pencil then painted carefully over each one. When his wife opened the bedroom door she'd asked if he was painting the Sistine Chapel.

He looked back at his men – they were filthy – each of them had red-rimmed eyes and cracked lips. He would miss them all. There was a time when he believed he was a lifer, a career soldier, but not now. These men were his second family. His real family was at home.

His men sat eating MREs from silver wrappers while complaining about the terrain.

– You know the Russians tried to come this way, said Figgs. Only they didn't make it.

– Alexander the Great's army before them, said Doc. They say the red-headed locals are descendants.

– Those old dudes dye their hair orange, said Figgs.

– And purple.

– How fucked up is that?

– What about the ones with purple beards, asked Figgs. Are they descendants?

They all laughed.

– Man, there's no way I want to get killed by some old dude with purple facial hair, said Figgs.

Fungi sat slightly apart from the other three, his weapon dismantled in front of him on an oil-stained green cloth. He was looking through one of the parts, blowing through it.

– Hey Fungi, asked Figgs. What're you gonna do when the war's over?

Fungi stopped for a minute.

– Look for another one. he said, before continuing to clean his weapon.

– This guy I know... a Recon Marine, said Figgs. He said they were somewhere up in Sangin. This local entrepreneur... he sets up a table beside a minefield... big knife, white butcher's coat, everything. He stands beside this minefield and waits. When a goat walks into the minefield and goes boom, he pays a kid to go in and get the meat.

– Like a goat kid? said Fungi.

– What?

– Ignore him, said Doc.

– Eat shit. Where was I?

– He pays the kid to go into the minefield.

– Yeah... he pays the kid. So these Marines were sick of eating MREs and they bought a bag of goat meat. That night they cooked up a stew and one of them Marines found a kid's hand in his stew.

– Man, that's sick.

– What did he do? asked Fungi.

– He ate it.

– Awesome.

– Okay guys, said Grice. We need to get moving.

Fungi immediately reassembled his weapon and they moved out.

*

It was the rising crows that told Kyam Mehadi they were coming. He opened the glass jar, picked the bullets out of the cloth, polished each one, blew on them, before slotting them individually into the magazine.

He had time. He slung the Lee Enfield over his shoulder and moved from his house, on wooden crutches, with great dexterity, along a smooth path to the very the edge of the cliff wall. From here he had a commanding view of the terrain, and there was only one way in.

At the top of three sets of wooden ladders he dropped his crutches – he would no longer need them – and slid down each ladder with practiced ease to the opening of the chosen house. Here, he had the best view. Once inside, he set up a firing position. His eyesight was still good. He thanked Allah for that.

When he was young, before the Russians came into the valley, the men of the village would each contribute to the purchase of a male goat, tether it to a wooden stake at a distance of around one thousand meters and then draw lengths of grass to see who would fire first. The first man to kill the goat kept it. His father had taught him how to get that first shot off accurately. And his family had eaten many goats.

When the Americans were twelve hundred meters away, he altered his breathing, his pulse steadied, the rifle became an extension of himself. He knew the exact distance, took into account the wind. One advantage of the metal sight was that he didn't have to raise his head, allowing him to remain hidden. He had the commander, the one giving instructions, in his sights. And he was sure he could make the shot; but it would be better to let them move closer.

Grice gave the clenched-fist hand signal to stop, looked up at the saddle and the almost vertical mountain wall to the left of it. To get to the summit it was necessary to move up through the steep saddle.

Like the previous village, the mountain was riddled with natural and man-made caves. There were no signs of life, but some of the cave entrances looked like they'd been maintained. He scanned slowly through the high-powered binoculars.

– Is this Hill 2020? asked Figgs.

– This is it, said Grice, without lowering the binoculars. This is what we trekked the whole way up here for.

– There's only one way in, said Fungi.

Each of the men was silent. They were all fully aware of what Fungi had just stated.

– How do we know there aren't any bad guys in that village? asked Figgs.

– We don't, said Grice.

Fungi pointed to the steppes on the saddle: Bad guys don't grow wheat.

– Yeah, said Doc. But they eat it.

– Keep an eye out for movement, said Grice.

The men moved up toward the village, keeping their spacing in case of ambush.

Grice felt the rush and heard the sound of a bullet passing by his right ear. Inches out.

– Contact, shouted Figgs. Sniper.

The men threw themselves into depressions in the terrain wherever they could, but they were all exposed.

– Anyone see anything? shouted Grice.

– Nothing.

– Fungi, said Grice. Put a couple of rounds into those caves.

He scuttled over, placed his outstretched arm, the

finger pointing, on Fungi's right shoulder.

– See the big one, there.

– Got it.

Fungi sat up, loaded the M4, aimed, and fired. The round lit up the cave house, setting fire to the wooden front.

– Another one, said Grice. There.

Fungi reloaded, hoisted the M4 to his shoulder, and fired. The explosive round missed the entrance and tore a hole in the granite wall of the cliff. Fungi cursed, tipped the front of his helmet back, and fired again, this time accurately lighting up the smaller cave entrance.

– You see anything, Figgs?

Figgs was scanning the vertical wall of rock through his high-powered sniper scope.

– No. Nothing. No movement.

Fungi fell backwards. He was dead before his head hit the ground: first the bullet then the sound of it. The round entered just above his right eye, tore through his skull, and knocked off his Kevlar helmet.

They all took cover where they could.

Grice looked down at Fungi. He couldn't take his eyes off the entrance wound. It seemed too small to kill a man. There was another shot. Grice felt and heard the sound of it passing by his left ear. Again, it had missed by an inch. Grice thought of his young son. He wanted to be with him, to spend the rest of his life with him, to help guide him through life.

– Anyone see anything?

– No, said Figgs. But I think it's a single sniper.

Doc scrambled over scattered stones to get Fungi's M4. Another echo. Doc was knocked clean off his feet and backwards by the impact. He felt a sharp pain in his chest. He checked for an entrance wound. There was none. The bullet had embedded in his body armor.

– Figgs, shouted Grice. Get an airstrike in, now!

– You got it.

Figgs called it in.

– Forty-five minutes, he shouted back to Grice.

– We need it now, yelled Grice. Right now!

As he shouted there was another shot. Figgs dropped the radio and screamed: I'm hit. I'm hit!

Doc scrambled over to him, held him down, and told him to be cool. The bullet had gone clean through his right shoulder. Doc packed it with Kerlix, but he didn't stick him with morphine, he needed him to be lucid. He would survive the injury, if they managed to get out. Figgs was lucky. If the bullet had nicked an artery this far out, he'd be dead before the medevac arrived.

Kyam Mehadi had one remaining bullet. Twice, he'd tried to get the commander. He adjusted his good leg until he was comfortable and offered up a prayer to Allah. He could see the man move as he shouted instructions to the radio operator. He waited until the commander's upper body was aligned with both metal sights. Then he fired.

The bullet stuck Grice's M4 and ricocheted up under his chin. He was still conscious when Doc Zanetti reached him. Doc forced Kerlix under his friend's bleeding chin. There was so much blood he couldn't see the full extent of the injury.

– Figgs, get back on that radio.

Doc injected his friend twice with morphine and turned to Figgs.

– We need a medevac.

Grice lay flat on his back. He imagined he was back home in the nursery he'd painted for his son. He looked up at the pale afternoon sky. He thought he could see a star.

Morgan Munn

Morgan Munn's brother cut him down. The body fell to the floor, a dead weight. When the ambulance arrived the body still had a pulse.

The hanging had robbed the brain of oxygen. The damage was permanent.

His brother understood why he had done it – and he felt the guilt of it – he also thought he would try to do it again.

His brother agreed he should be sectioned.

Morgan Munn spent the next six months in a secure mental health unit.

Upon release, his brother paid for a room within the grounds of a private trust.

Morgan Munn acquired a shopping trolley.

He wheeled the trolley through the grounds of the Trust and onto the footpath, then along the road to the hospital shop. And he filled the trolley with bottles of cola. He filled the trolley until it could take no more.

Many visitors came to recognise him and paused to think; to wonder at his pathetic shape: the head tilted, the vacant, but not unkindly look on his face.

His teeth became black stumps from drinking all that cola.

As he lay in bed, his brother would stroke his wild mane of hair and rub Bonjela on his gums.

Some nights, when he knew they were alone, his brother would get on his knees at the side of the bed and beg him for forgiveness.

And Morgan Munn would hum, at peace with the world.

Vainglory
After Paul Bowles

Under the cliff's shade, a flamingo stood on one leg in a shallow pool staring at his own reflection. He remained in this pose, until he heard something approaching.

The swinging head of a hyena appeared through the tough grass. When the hyena reached the water's edge he stood, two front paws in the water, and drank.

His thirst satisfied, he lifted his large head.

– I've never seen a flamingo at this pool.

The flamingo stepped back slightly, into the deeper water.

– Are you afraid of me?

– No, I'm not afraid.

– Good, then we can talk as equals.

– I'm returning home, said the flamingo, quickly.

– To the soda lake at Isenegeza?

– Yes, said the flamingo. You should visit the soda lake.

– I would need your coat of feathers.

The hyena knew the leopard had already tried. He also knew he'd died a slow death, his paws shackled with crystals of soda.

– It's not far.

– But too far for me, said the hyena.

Then he asked the flamingo what he'd seen on his journey.

The flamingo talked easily about himself until most of the daylight had risen into the night sky. Suddenly, he realised it was almost dark. He flapped his wings and moved up towards the escarpment.

– Why are you leaving, said the hyena. Can't you see in the dark?

– I know there are seven deadly sins... and you are afflicted by them all!

The hyena listened, his head cocked to one side, until he heard the flamingo's body strike the cliff wall.

As the hyena climbed up over the boulders, the flamingo lay shivering.

– There were once eight deadly sins, said the hyena.

– I know of only seven.

– The eighth of them was vainglory.

Quickly, he seized the flamingo's neck, tearing out the feathers to get at the soft flesh.

When his belly was full, he rolled in the feathers and gore.

Momentarily, he stood laughing at how ridiculous he looked in his pink-feathered coat. Then he thanked God for eyes that could see in the dark and were not blinded by his own reflection.

Boom Boom

Tomas 'Boom Boom' DeGale was a promising super-middleweight, with a pro record of nine and zero. He was twenty-three years old, worked in the 7-Eleven, and lived with his mother and younger sister.

His sister was seventeen. She'd just met a guy twice her age.

DeGale called to see him, told him to stay away from his kid sister.

His sister arrived home crying, bruised and bleeding.

When DeGale had finished, the guy was put on life support.

DeGale had no criminal record, but the guy had almost died.

He was given four years in the State Pen.

The sixth floor was for inmates who had committed violent crimes. It was an open cell – a dormitory – housing forty-eight men. There were two toilets for those forty-eight men.

When things got quiet, DeGale would read *The Ring* magazine.

He'd been there a week. Three guys stood round his bunk. The rolled-up sleeves and V-neck of their orange prison vests revealed masses of blue-black prison ink.

DeGale swung his legs around and put both bare feet on the prison floor.

– What you get? asked the one directly in front of him.

– What I get? I got four years.

– Long time, man... long time on your own.

One of them picked up *The Ring*.

– You like to box?

The biggest of them began shadowboxing – his stance and balance all wrong.

– I said, you like to box?

DeGale looked from the big shadowboxer to the guy standing over him.

– Put the magazine down.

The guy hit DeGale hard. He rolled backwards with the punch, off the bed, and landed on his feet.

He was filled with adrenaline now.

The same guy made a move for him. DeGale let him come and hit him square on the chin.

When the big shadowboxer took a shot, he took

it and countered with a blow to the side of the guy's head.

Now the third guy threw a punch. DeGale feinted, and immediately connected with a series of combinations, first to the body and then to the head.

The remainder of the fight was a mixture of wrestling and DeGale using his boxing skill when he got a bit of distance between himself and the three of them.

He woke up in the infirmary.

Both hands were so swollen he couldn't make a fist. He got up off the bunk slowly, walked to the sink, filled it with cold water.

For a full ten minutes he stood there, bent over, his hands in the water. He was a quick healer: in a week, ten days, he'd be good.

He was given a standard prison questionnaire, with tick boxes and dotted lines, where an inmate might like to elaborate. He ticked the box saying he couldn't identify his assailants.

When he got out of the infirmary, an older guy came to see him. The guy was calm. He had presence.

– Four years, huh, he said.

– This place is a fucking zoo.

The man cleared his throat.

– The prison administration states that having

inmates live this way encourages cooperation and healthy peer relationships.

DeGale didn't smile.

– I could use someone like you.

– I'm no killer.

The man laughed.

– Then you're the only one in here who isn't. I don't need a killer.

He pointed over to a little guy who sat on a bunk, across the dorm, watching. The guy had three teardrops on his face. Each teardrop represented a life he'd taken while inside.

– If I wanted someone killed, I could send Donzo with a blade. No... I just want you to beat up on someone. That's all you have to do.

– That's it? said DeGale.

– Just mark him, show we got to him.

– And after that?

– After that you can lie back and read *The Ring*.

– Who's the guy?

– He's not on this floor.

– I'm not interested in gangs, said DeGale. I just want to do my time and get out of here.

– You change your mind, you come see me... my name's Harlan.

DeGale wrote a letter to his mother telling her he

was in fear for his life.

His mother phoned the prison administration, was put on hold, told it would be looked into, that there was due process.

His mother came to visit.

It was a six-hour round trip on public transport.

She was shocked to see the state of her son.

De Gale told his mother he was fine; he just needed her to write a letter to the governor.

His mother wrote the letter that day.

Within a week he was moved to the fifth floor

It took him three days to get the guy. Mostly he hit him on either side of the eyes, marking him, but he didn't do any lasting damage.

DeGale was put in segregation for a month.

When he got out, he was moved back up to the sixth floor. His new bunk was below Harlan's. On the bed were two copies of *The Ring*. The men became good friends. DeGale learned things about human nature. He also learned that a bit of him had died.

He asked his mother and little sister not to visit. He asked them to write.

When he was released, his mother looked him up and down and asked: What have they done to you, Tomas?

His little sister hugged him. She couldn't stop

talking... she had a new partner, two kids... she said how unfair it was he had to do the whole four years... she told him she loved him, she felt so guilty... she thought his shaved head and goatee suited him... she liked the ink on his arms... she didn't like the single teardrop on his face, but she was glad prison hadn't changed him.

The only one

In mid-afternoon, during the worst heat of the day, Swing walked quickly through the front doors of Zane Hipsy Secure Mental Health Unit in downtown Austin, following eighteen months of what they termed 'psychodynamic psychotherapy'.

For a brief moment he stood there under the blue sky, taking in the buildings, the sound of traffic, the smell of exhaust fumes, before opening the door of a waiting cab. The cab took him to his ex-wife's on Arroyo Blanco. The house had, for a time, belonged to them both but she'd bought him out after the divorce. While the cab waited, he tried the garage door; it was locked, so he opened it with the only key he owned, lifted it up halfway, and bent under.

To get inside the garage he had to climb over a trailer. In the trailer were various things: paint cans, a travel case, his old fishing chair, and a little pink tricycle with white tires. The tricycle belonged to his daughter; he'd bought it for her when she was little.

He looked around for something to stand on. There

was a plastic cool-box sitting on the floor beside his power saw. He stood on the cool-box, reached up under the beams of the garage roof, between the heating pipes and the insulation, and pulled his old army duffel bag through a gap in the pipes.

Inside the bag was his driver's license, twelve thousand dollars cash, a credit card with a limit of five thousand dollars, and a Sig Sauer 9mm.

From the trailer, he lifted out the travel case, unzipped it and placed everything inside, lifted the cooler, and placed it on top of the travel case before wheeling everything to the cab.

The cab dropped him off downtown at Alamo car rental and he tipped the driver ten bucks.

Outside he stopped, broke the foil on one large red pill, placed it into his mouth, and swallowed before walking inside with the case trailing behind him.

Momentarily he stood in the cool of the air-conditioned office.

– Can I help you, sir?

He stood staring at nothing, before answering.

– I want to hire a car.

– Have you a particular car in mind?

– I want a Mustang. A ragtop.

– Ford Mustang, yessir.

The guy scrolled the screen.

– Sir, we're currently out of Mustangs. We should have one in tomorrow.

– Tomorrow's no good.

– We have the Sebring convertible. Good car. Chrysler been running the show in family drop tops for the past fifteen years.

– Do I look like family?

His shoulder was beginning to hurt; right through the bone and out the other side.

– There's one right out front, said the guy.

Swing opened the door and stood looking around the parking lot.

– The white one?

– That's it.

– Okay, I'll take it.

– And for how long, sir?

– Three days.

– I can offer you fully comprehensive, total-peace-of-mind insurance—

– Just standard is fine.

The guy processed his details.

– Have you something planned?

– Oh yeah, said Swing, but that was all he said.

Outside, he lifted the travel case, and as he did so, the handle came away in his hand. He turned the case on its side and noticed for the first time it was missing a wheel, and it occurred to him. The things he'd seen in the trailer were the things his ex-wife's new partner was taking to the junkyard. He thought of the tricycle he'd bought for his daughter, and he felt an overwhelming rage.

He got in the car and drove. He didn't know how long he drove for. When the rage blew out, he was somewhere on Alte Verde. He needed to find a drugstore; he remembered one on Eastside.

He parked out back of a neon sign that said *Prescriptions,* walked in dragging the case behind him, down one aisle to the counter, the 9mm held in front.

– Put your hands above your head and keep them there...

The pharmacist put both hands straight up in the air.

– Now push that camera up to the ceiling.

– Camera doesn't work.

– Push it up to the ceiling anyway.

The pharmacist did as he was told.

– I only work here. Take what you want.

– I don't need money. I need drugs.

He paused.

– Two hundred fast release Oxycodone at sixty mil each... and two hundred ten mil Xanax...

The pharmacist stared at him, mouth open.

– Like, fucking now...

– You got it.

Then Swing remembered the nausea the Oxy-codone caused.

– And something for nausea.

– You feeling sick?

– Not now, no, but it's the Oxys.

– Have you tried Dramamine?

– Maybe, said Swing. I been on *that* much shit.

– Well, they're good, no drowsiness. I take them for IBS. Take one every three hours. Then he said: I'll add some Windeze, just take if and when...

– Thank you, said Swing. Appreciate it.

When the pharmacist got the drugs, Swing pointed at the wheeled case and the guy bent down, placed them inside and zipped it.

– I hear a siren I'll come back and kill you. No offence.

He walked out pulling the broken travel case behind him, like he was going on vacation.

Before moving on to the highway he pulled up at Spec's Liquor store on Ennis. As he walked inside, the floor squeaked. He stopped, looked at some beers. The guy behind the cash register looked at him, and he was stood there stuck to the floor looking at beer he didn't want, then he saw a big stainless-steel slicer and a block of cheese.

– You got a deli counter? he asked, all surprised.

The guy wore a white V-neck T-shirt he was busting out of.

– Uh huh, got it in last year.

– I need some cheese and ham.

The guy placed both his palms on the counter and leaned forward.

– We have some good specialty cheeses... I'd recommend the Ubriaco... it's an Italian... soaked in local wine the last six months.

Swing felt the pain shoot down his right arm and remain as a tingling in his fingers.

– Just regular ham and cheddar... one pound of each, sliced.

As the ham and cheese were sliced, Swing lifted a bag of ice out of a chest freezer and carried it to the counter.

– That everything?

– Two bottles of Wild Turkey and three soft-packs of Marlboro Red.

While he waited, he held open his wallet, and there in a little square of see-thru plastic, was the only photograph he had of his daughter. It was taken when she was six months old. He'd come back from Iraq and there she was. Now he wasn't allowed access; the county court judge had made that very clear. He wished he had a photograph of her now; in his head he carried an image of a little blonde six-year-old with pigtails.

– Your change, sir.

– Wha...

– Your change.

– Oh yeah. Thanks.

Swing got in the car, put everything in the cool-box, took another red pill and drove.

He drove, sipping the Wild Turkey from the bottle, necking pills, the wind roaring in his ears, his head, and he felt a euphoria that lasted for miles.

In front, where the long straight road ran right through the clouds, buzzards rode the slow thermals and the road dipped directly through perfectly cut slabs of flat rock, bordered by barrel cactus, scrub, and desert. And he passed a sign that said:

Welcome to New Mexico
The Land of Enchantment

The sign had a red and green chili on it someone had used for target practice.

He drove on past, and through some low mountains full of gypsum dunes that looked like snowdrifts. Then the light dimmed as big gray and crimson clouds broiled and rolled up from the earth. And it rained. Swing gunned the engine and moved over the sheets of water that ran from the road until he came out the other side and into hot sunshine, and he felt an abrupt and overwhelming fatigue.

Within a mile he saw a sign for the Sunburst Motel. He pulled in and parked outside another sign that said *Office* in big red letters. Sitting behind a reinforced glass window was a black dude.

– I need a single room for one night.

– Forty bucks for one night and forty bucks deposit.

When he said bucks, he lisped, and Swing saw one of his front teeth was missing.

– It's a hot one, said Swing.

– Sure is... you got room number five.

Swing peeled off four twenty-dollar bills and the guy placed the key on one of those stainless-steel trays you get in all-night gas stations.

– You get any of that there rain?

– Hasn't rained anywhere around here in months, mister.

Swing stood there with the key in his hand, without blinking, wondering how the hell the guy hadn't seen all that rain.

– There anywhere round here I can eat? he said, eventually.

– Turn left, walk to the end of the block.

He turned and looked across to the motel pool

where white plastic chairs lay scattered on their sides like they'd been kicked over, and there was a big broad-leafed palm, and the dead leaves had blown up underneath it, and some of those leaves floated on the water. And something about those dead leaves triggered the hyper-vigilance that had become such a feature of his life. Immediately, he was aware of ambush positions. On the roof, on the ground, in front of him, behind him, everywhere.

– Where's my room?

– Number five, said the guy, pointing to his right. Ground floor.

Swing moved to his left, keeping his profile as low as possible, while trailing the case, the cool-box on top, moving from one firing point to the next, remembering what he'd been taught, how he'd lived – fire and maneuver – and he felt the pain in the muscle, the bone, the nerves.

He made it to the room, locked the door, pulled the curtains, and sat to the left of the window with the Sig in his hand. He sat there until, slowly, things receded. He took a handful of pills, drank some cool bourbon from the bottle, lay down on the floor, and passed out.

When he woke the next morning, he looked around the room and there was a delay between what he looked at and what he saw, and he knew he would have that feeling all day.

He walked to the bathroom and stood under the shower, his flat palms against the tiles, looking at the water as it drained down the plug.

In the bedroom, he remembered the cheese and ham. It was submerged in cool water, but it was fine. He rolled up his sleeve and pulled it out, making Scoobie snacks, minus the bread.

Then he got in the car and drove.

Some way out he remembered he'd forgotten his deposit, but he wasn't going back for it. He took the Aqua Fria Freeway on to the US 93. Once in Nevada, he took the Las Vegas exit at number 75, drove without stopping until he saw the Stratosphere in the distance.

He cruised along the Strip and into the Venetian; right up to the front doors, gave the boy his key and accepted his ticket. Someone reached forward to take his case and cool-box, but Swing kept walking – almost knocking the guy over – to the reception desk.

At the desk, no one called him, so he looked up at the high-domed glass ceiling, and it shot up into the sky in a chase of crystal. And he followed that crystal on a meteor trail.

– Sir, can I help you?

– I'd like a room.

He produced his credit card and was given a room on the seventh floor.

As he made his way to the elevators, he was stopped by a big guy in a brown security uniform who was paid to remember faces. Swing flashed his white key card and the guy waved him through.

He took the elevator to the seventh floor then walked down a long newly carpeted corridor to his room.

The room was on two levels. On the higher level he tried the bed. It was firm and it was good.

He stepped down to the lower level and took in the view of Vegas. He could see right along the strip. In the bright sunlight it looked beautiful. He turned and knelt in front of the safe. It asked for a six-digit code. Swing knew he would forget any code. Then he remembered his daughter's date of birth and typed in 10-12-02 in red digital.

Twenty minutes later, he was sat at the pool drinking Hofmeister.

Two kids stopped – shaved heads, fresh tattoos – and they recognized his own tattoos.

– Hey man, we ask you something?

Swing just stared at them.

– You army?

– I was.

– Hey bro, my name's Coot, this here's my buddy Chris. We signed up at Fort Worth.

Swing continued to stare.

– We're waiting to be deployed. This is our last hurrah.

Half an hour later, and Swing was on a roll; it was the Hofmeister and the drugs and meeting the two kids.

– Me, I'm a born adrenaline junkie, addicted to excitement; that's why I signed up in the first place. I read about it in the hospital. Then he looked over at the pool and said: I can swim a length underwater... twenty bucks. I'll bet you twenty bucks I can do it.

The two kids looked at the swimming pools.

– The fifty meter pool?

Swing knew there was a time he might have made the fifty meter pool, but not now.

– The thirty meter pool.

One of them said: You gotta kick off. No diving.

– They don't let you dive, said Swing.

– Okay. Twenty bucks.

Swing took off his shirt, and they saw the damage. The right shoulder was scarred and the muscle on the upper right arm was wasted, and they no longer wanted to talk about war, and they didn't think it was a fair bet.

When he eased into the water it felt like his blood was chilled. Maybe he'd had too much sun. He rested his back against the edge of the pool, took a deep breath, went under, and kicked off. It was different under the water; it was cool and his skin prickled and he was drawn to the faint patches of sudden white light on the bottom.

He felt his heartbeat pumping in his ears. Then, beyond halfway, he felt an overwhelming urge to breathe, but he fought it with everything he had and he kept pushing toward the other end because he wanted to win that bet and he wanted to prove he was still the person he'd always been, that nothing had changed him, that war hadn't changed him, that the death of his buddies hadn't changed him, that not being allowed access to his daughter hadn't changed him.

He was almost there when he heard a child calling out to him; it sounded slow and far away. He opened his mouth in reply, and he felt himself taken to a bright pool of clear water.

He was hauled out.

A lifeguard pumped him, and there at the side of the pool, two gallons of Hofmeister, pool water, and what looked like cheese and ham gushed out. As the lifeguard pumped, the heart compressed, and through muscle memory or some random act of God, it began to beat. As it beat, blood ran to his brain, synapses sparked, neurons ran like lightning, and he was speaking.

– Get the fuck offa me!

When he eventually stood up, the two kids had gone.

He walked to his room and slept.

Later, he was sat at a card table wearing a black-and-gold Hawaiian shirt a size too big that he didn't remember buying. It was a hold'em cash game and he had a stack. The dealer nodded to him, and he pushed all in.

A guy at the end of the table looked at him, looked at his cards, and said: What the hell, I call.

The dealer burned and turned, and the guy hit a nine of spades on the river for the gutshot.

– Unlucky, said the guy, reaching both hands out and pulling in all the chips.

Swing just sat there.

– Unlucky, he said.

And he felt a pain worse than the pain in his shoulder, right up through his balls and into his throat.

– Sir, would you like to buy in again? asked the dealer.

– Unlucky, said Swing. Un-fucking-lucky.

– Sir, I will have to ask you to refrain from using

profanity at the table.

Swing stood up, looked at the guy who'd just won the hand, and said: Stay here, buddy.

Then he made his way through the slot machines, past the blackjack tables, and the big security guy in the brown uniform who knew his face by now.

The elevator doors opened, he stepped in and pressed seven. The elevator stopped on the second floor and a little blonde-haired girl in pigtails stepped in carrying a snorkel, mask, and towel. She pressed five, stood back, and they both waited there in the elevator.

When the elevator stopped at five the door opened, and the little girl stepped forward, then walked away.

Swing was stood there alone, and he watched her go until the doors closed completely.

At seven he stepped through the doors and walked to his room.

He knelt down at the safe, typed in his daughter's date of birth, opened it, took out the Sig, removed the magazine, checked it, replaced it in the butt of the weapon, pushed the mag tight with the heel of his hand, released the safety catch, placed it in his mouth, and pulled the trigger.

Gutshot

J ust out of range is the white bull buffalo. He has seen this animal before, in dreams.

Cradling his rifle, he crawls on his belly through the sweet grass.

With this same rifle he learned to shoot at Cemetery Ridge, taking Confederate soldiers from a distance of two hundred yards. In those three days of slaughter he knows exactly how many men he killed. At night, each pallid face comes to visit.

The warm breeze is in his favor, and it brings with it that peculiar bovine smell, like freshly dug earth and sulfur springs.

Patiently, he waits for the bull to come to him, but the herd changes direction, slowly moving further out of range.

If he takes the shot now, it will be the longest he's ever made. He presses the curved Kentucky-style stock into his shoulder and takes the shot.

Almost immediately, from a full six hundred yards, the large bore bullet rips through the bull's taut white belly. His squat back legs drop, and he staggers, confused, quick-stepping now toward his cows and calves, the red already spreading.

The sound of the shot travels far across the sea of grass and into the land of the Comanche.

Two bulls at the front of the herd break into a gallop, the remainder of the herd follows. The white bull is somewhere in the middle.

Gutshot like that, he will take a full day to die.

Holding the long rifle in one hand, he stands upright in the cool grass, watching the herd thunder toward the distant horizon. Their collective movement shakes the ground he stands on.

Cursing his stupidity, he makes his way back to his hobbled pony.

It isn't the hide that interests him now – he feels sick in his stomach knowing he's made a terrible mistake – he simply can't allow the bull to die like that.

Inspector Singh's dog

Manish Singh had studied at the London School of Economics. After graduation he returned to India to marry. Although the marriage had been arranged by his family, he was delighted with his young bride; she was very pretty, if a little fragile.

Upon return from honeymoon, he joined the Mumbai police force. As a graduate he was fast-tracked to promotion and quickly made it to the rank of inspector. He brought his meticulous administrative skills to the job, met budgets, and showed a talent for delegation.

The promotion allowed for a move to a large house in a gated community. His neighbours were now lawyers, judges, and politicians. From the bedroom window was a wonderful view of the city, while the back of the house overlooked the lush green of virgin forest.

When Singh and his wife moved in to their beautiful new house, they were eager to start a family. But his wife was unable to conceive. They tried every possible remedy, from traditional cures to expensive in-vitro fertilisation. Eventually, they quietly accepted their fate.

In the months that followed, Singh bought an English bulldog. The animal cost an extortionate sum. When the weaned pup first arrived it was already a sturdy animal, with a massive head. Singh – much to his wife's disapproval – named the dog Jaws.

However, as the dog grew to adulthood Singh came to realise that Jaws was no guard dog. Sometimes the animal showed an interest when visitors rang the electric bell at the tall wrought-iron gates. On other occasions it simply lay in the shade of the aparajita tree, large head on folded paws, snoring, while the visitors waited outside the gate.

Each morning after the inspector left for work, his wife brought Jaws into the cool of the house, and it sat beside her on the sofa as she read the English glamour magazines. Singh's wife renamed it George.

The morning George vanished, Inspector Singh walked quietly downstairs to the kitchen, filled the kettle, and opened the back door. As always, he took two eggs from a brass bowl. One for himself and one for George. Normally George would be waiting at the door for his boiled egg. However, this morning when Singh opened the door the dog wasn't there. He called the dog's name, left the kitchen door open, and returned to the boiling kettle. When he'd finished adding the boiled water to the pan, and placed it on the heated ring, he walked outside.

All around the house he walked calling George's name, but there was no sign of his dog.

He hurried back into the house and shouted upstairs to his wife (who always slept late).

– Where's George? I can't find George.

His wife didn't answer. She was asleep.

He rushed back outside and looked again in the kennel. George wasn't there. Again, he walked around the walled garden, this time at pace. Nothing. The iron gates were locked, and it wasn't possible for George to dig underneath: he was arthritic and on painkillers.

The inspector ran upstairs to his wife, shook her awake, then immediately drove to work in a hurry.

At his office he summoned Detective Malik. There was very little happening in the local underworld that escaped Malik's attention. Inspector Singh was merely a figurehead; it was Detective Malik and his men who dealt with the local gangsters.

As the inspector relayed George's mystery disappearance, Malik took out a notebook and when he thought it appropriate, scribbled notes. When the inspector had finished, Malik stood up and told his boss he would have news by the end of the day.

That afternoon Malik reported back to Singh. George had been found hanging in a neighbour's garden, the dog's large head wedged between the forked branches of a large Parajita tree.

Singh's fury was matched only by his grief. He told Malik to round up the suspects.

Malik had two police vans at his disposal. He and his men packed each van with gangsters.

Singh stayed late that night and into the early morning. He sat on a high-backed chair of black bamboo, watching as each of the local gangsters was interrogated and beaten.

Each man gave the names of other men. They, in turn, were loaded into the police vans and brought into the station for interrogation. But no one knew who had committed such a despicable act.

Eventually, the men were released.

In the coming weeks the local crime rate plummeted. As Singh drove past the traders on his way to and from work, they stood behind their colourful stalls, staring. He was sure the marketplace – normally such a hive of criminal activity – was now a much quieter place.

The beatings had earned the inspector a newfound respect from his staff, the local population, and most particularly from the criminal gangs. However, the crime remained unsolved.

Months later, Singh sat down with a single egg for breakfast to read an article in the *Mumbai Times*.

A recent scientific study states the number of pariah dogs has soared by seven million in recent years. The increasing number of dogs has drawn leopards into the city to prey upon them. The leopard will often wedge the dog in the bough of a tree, before returning later to feed...

Inspector Singh placed the newspaper on the table, took off his reading glasses, and called upstairs to his wife. But she didn't answer. She was asleep.

Tim Coatchilli

The next morning Coatchilli woke shivering in the desert. The sun was rising. He stood up, cupped his hands around his eyes, and scanned the ground ahead. There was nothing here, not even the remains of things.

To the south were rounded red hills. He was sure he could find water there. He looked to the hills, made a decision, and set off walking in their direction.

Often, as a child, he would walk with his grandfather with a distant object in view, wondering if he would ever reach it. On walkabout, Coatchilli would carry a hardwood spear and a wooden pitchi for water. His grandfather would carry many things.

Now, as he headed for the hills, there were things he saw. The contours of the land, the tracks of goanna and roo. On one of the trails he picked up some dry roo dung and placed it in the pocket of his trouser. It could be used to start a fire. Many years before his grandfather had shown him how.

After his grandfather died, Coatchilli was sent

to a white school. His father was a white fella and Coatchilli had inherited his green eyes. And, with his hair cut short, he looked like a white boy, but he wasn't a white boy. At school, he would sit in the class-room following the sun's arc through the sky until the bell rang. In the playground he would fight. Then, later, in the outback bars. And, after each fight, when he had time to reflect, he would relive the violence and feel the pain of it.

When he reached the red hills, he found a rock overhang. His people had used this place many times. Inside, he found the remains of a fire and some dry wood. Beside the ashes was an empty soup tin; perfect for carrying water. The tin was rusty but sound. He cleaned it up with sand, wobbling the sharp lid backwards and forwards until it broke free. This simple, concerted effort had him light-headed. He needed water.

Outside the overhang, the gradient was gentle, the smooth red surface easy on his bare feet. Where two adjoining pieces of sloping rock met, he found water in a cleft. He knelt down, tied a knot in the cuff of his shirt-sleeve, and filled the sleeve with the cool water, suspending it above his mouth where the pure drops filtered through the fabric. He filled the tin can the same way and sat looking at the sky. Soon it would be dark; he would need a fire.

Inside the overhang, he sat down on the cool sand and tried to remember how his grandfather had made fire. He fashioned one of his bootlaces and a springy green branch into a loose bow. Then he sharpened a thin, dry stick with the old tin lid and rolled the point in the hollow of a larger piece of hardwood. For a long time he persevered, but there was no more than a wisp of smoke; no ember and no fire. Soon his fingers became swollen and cut and they began to blister. He tried to concentrate on what his grandfather had taught him, but his thoughts raced too fast.

He lay down on the cool, red floor of the overhang, shaking. He had suffered the horrors many times before, but there was nothing familiar about this. As his body convulsed, he remembered his grandfather's story about a man and his son crossing the desert, when the son got sick. The father built his son a shelter for protection and went away to look for food. When the father returned the shelter was empty. He looked everywhere but his son was gone. Leaning against a tree, the father looked up and saw a cocoon and pupa dangling directly above his head, and he knew then that the spirits had saved his son by turning him into a pupa.

Back then, the story had frightened Coatchilli,

but his grandfather had reassured him. There was nothing to fear; the land, the animals, and the people were one.

For the next three nights he carried black rocks from the desert and built a cocoon within the shelter. The black rocks retained the heat from the sun and got him through the cold nights.

On the third night he dreamed of making fire. When he woke, he remembered. *Start with a drill stick as straight as possible.* He searched until he found the right stick. He used the sharp tin lid to shave off the bark. He took his time. It was the first time in a long time he had taken his time with anything. When he was satisfied the stick was clean, he sharpened the drill end.

Adjusting the loose bow, he slackened the bootlace to accommodate the drill stick, rolling it backwards and forwards, practising. Then he made a small depression in the hardwood to take the point of the drill stick. It was all coming back to him. He marveled at the skills he imagined he had forgotten.

As Coatchilli's left foot pinned down the end to be drilled, he positioned a ball of dry roo dung under the drill point and began a gentle sawing motion. *Don't hold your breath or you'll become exhausted. If you saw too quickly, you'll lose control.* That's what his grandfather had said in the dream.

When it began to smoke, he continued sawing in smooth, rhythmic strokes until he had the glimmer of a coal. Then, wrapping the glowing coal in the dry roo dung, he blew on it until he had a flame.

That night, Coatchilli slept beside a warm fire.

Shortly after dawn he woke, desperately needing a drink. The urge came from deep within. He set off towards the settlement. He cursed himself for throwing away his coins, but he could beg outside the bottleshops.

He walked at pace, his head racing with nonsense thoughts. He hated the name Coatchilli. He had wanted to be called Armstrong or Fletcher like the white kids at school. Later, in the outback bars he grew to loathe his Christian name, Tim. It was a white man's name, a weak name.

Eventually he sat down in the hot sand.

At his feet, ants busied themselves. He looked closely at them. They were honeypot soldier ants. If he could find the workers, he could take their honey. He traced the soldiers to tiny holes in the dry ground, then scraped away the parched surface with his fingertips until he came across the vertical shaft of the nest. Then he searched for a hardwood stick with which he could dig. When he found something suitable, he dug down until he was at the nest. There he picked up the large honeypot workers. They looked like miniature grapes with heads and legs attached; the swollen amber abdomens filled with honey. He picked them up individually and nipped off the honeypot bellies with his front teeth. The taste of sugar helped satisfy his craving for alcohol.

When he could eat no more, he sat for a while in the sand. His grandfather had looked like a honeypot ant when he died – the bloated belly, the stick-like limbs.

Coatchilli looked back the way he had come, then he looked in the direction of the settlement. He wanted to go back to the desert, but the need to drink had returned.

Reluctantly, he stood and began walking towards the settlement. As he walked, he remembered his childhood. At white school he had learned about the Bible. He remembered how Jesus had gone walkabout for forty days without eating. When he told his grandfather this story, his grandfather told him about the powerful spirits who created the land and people during the Dreamtime. They were here before men or animals, plants or any other thing. And he told him about the Great Creator, the

Rainbow Serpent, protector of the land and the people. His grandfather told him that, during the Dreamtime, the Rainbow Serpent set off to look for his own tribe, shaping the land with his massive body as he went, gouging out river channels and throwing up mountain ranges. As the Rainbow Serpent searched for his own people, he listened for the wind but heard only voices jabbering in strange languages.

As Coatchilli continued he recognised many features in the landscape. Nothing had changed. He spotted a rocky outcrop and remembered it as a special place. He climbed up there, located the painting on the rock wall, and placed his palm on a handprint. It fitted perfectly. As a boy he had done the same thing, but his hand was too small. He remembered wishing he was big, as big as his grandfather.

When Coatchilli reached the ridge above the settlement, he stopped and looked down at the buildings; there was a storm in the distance, a rainbow had formed. It reminded him of the rest of the story. The Rainbow Serpent searched for his own people. When he found them, they were singing and dancing. The Rainbow Serpent watched, unsure of what to do. But, when he eventually showed himself, his own kind welcomed him.

Coatchilli fell to his knees and prayed. He pleaded with the wind and the rain, and the moon and the stars, and Jesus, and the Rainbow Serpent to free him from his sickness.

And he slept – a deep, dreamless sleep.

When he woke, he felt different; the need to drink had been plucked out of him. He looked at the land and he saw the things that were there. Then he looked down at the settlement, and finally under-stood who he was. He was Tim Coatchilli.

Something happened

You wait to speak with the priest. When he finally arrives you can't bring yourself to say anything.

You hurry out, the harsh sound of your heels resounding in the small church.

Outside, you stand in the sunlight, breathless.

Then you get back in the car and drive.

It's only when the fuel light comes on that you stop. At a petrol station you fill the tank.

You decide to head south, across the border.

For hours you drive, through farmland and rolling fields of flowering rape-seed that make your eyes water, through small towns and backroads, until something within you settles.

At a small village you park the car.

There's a main street. Nothing else.

In the street, beside a patch of barren ground, is a pub with an old faded Gallagher's Cigarettes sign on the gable wall.

Inside the small bar, it's dim. You remain at the open door waiting for your eyes to fully adjust. Sitting on barstools are two other customers. Old men with their caps on.

They both look at you.

The barman says hello.

– Hello, you reply.

– And what can I get you?

– I'll have a crème de menthe and white lemonade.

– Well now, he says, I've got the white lemonade, but I wouldn't sell too much of the crème de menthe.

You look to the shelf of spirits.

– A Pernod and white is good.

– Sure you are.

Some hours later, you stand in the dark under an umbrella. The rain is heavy. You don't recognise the umbrella.

A man is changing the driver's side wheel of your car.

On the skinned knuckles of his right hand there is blood and a black mark from the tyre. He wears torn yellow waterproofs. The torn hood draped over his head.

– Excuse me, you say. Can you tell me what happened?

Six in total

A young man by the name of Zahafian had reported the killing of his older brother by wolves. Normally, Sergeant Hamad would assign the case to one of his juniors, but he decided to investigate this one himself. It would prove to the men he was still more than capable of doing the hard miles. Also, no one believed the story about wolves, and the crime scene was only four miles from a tavern that made the most amazing meat and barley stew.

The sergeant rode out early on a big dun mare called Juno. His destination was twenty miles away, but he wasn't a skilled horseman. He considered horses a means of transport along tracks that couldn't accommodate an all-terrain vehicle.

He covered the distance well, stopping only twice to relieve himself and stretch out his legs and back. While he relaxed, the mare grazed on shoots that bordered the dirt road.

When Hamad arrived at the stone cottage, he took his rifle from the scabbard by the saddle. A young man, unshaven and wild-eyed, came out to greet him and introduced himself as Engin Zahafian. They went inside and the sergeant asked for the details of the killing.

– My brother Arif was bigger than me. He always carried the axe when we went to the forest, and I carried the bundles back to the house. Two days ago we'd been cutting wood for an hour when we saw a black wolf.

The sergeant nodded, scribbled the date in his notepad.

– Looking at that black wolf was like looking at the devil himself. I raised my arms and shouted, but the beast had no fear. A minute later another one appeared.

Hamad wrote the words 'black dog'.

– My brother raised the axe to them, but they weren't frightened. They charged at my brother and four more wolves appeared from nowhere to join the attack. They were all upon him. I was terrified and ran to the house to fetch our gun. When I came back there was no sign of Arif or the wolves.

– Were you injured? asked the sergeant.

– No, I was lucky.

– Indeed. Can you take me to the scene of the attack?

The young man got up from the table and reached above the fireplace for a shotgun.

– You won't need that, said Hamad.

Zahafian paused, then headed to the door and set off towards the forest. Hamad hung back a couple of paces, his rifle nestled in the crook of his arm. When they arrived at the clearing Hamad noted stains that could have been blood.

– And how many wolves did you say there were? he asked.

– I counted six.

– Six, said the sergeant.

He took out his notepad but wrote nothing.

The sergeant had seen enough. He walked back to his horse and carefully slotted the rifle into its scabbard beside the saddle.

– What will happen now? asked Zahafian.

– I'll draw up a report.

In fact, he was planning on producing an arrest warrant for murder.

– And someone will come to hunt down the wolves?

Hamad mounted his mare.

– Oh yes... someone will be here as soon as I complete my report.

On his way back to the station Hamad stopped at the tavern, choosing a table in the corner. The innkeeper fussed around, wiping the solid oak table top, complimenting the sergeant, asking why he didn't visit more often. Hamad said he'd been working on some high-profile cases.

– And is it business or pleasure today?

– Business, said Hamad.

The innkeeper set him up a cold pitcher of beer and returned minutes later with a steaming bowl of meat and barley stew. When Hamad finished his meal, he asked the man to sit with him.

– Did you hear about the death of the older Zahafian brother?

– Everyone's talking about it, said the innkeeper.

– Have you ever seen wolves in the area?

– No, never.

– What do you know about the brothers?

– Like normal brothers, said the innkeeper. Sometimes they came in and drank, occasionally they fought. Normal.

The sergeant wrote this down in his notepad.

– Thank you for your time, he said.

The innkeeper set down another pitcher of beer, which Hamad finished quickly.

When he got up to pay, the innkeeper refused, told him it was his honour.

Hamad strode to his mare. It was much later than he

realised, and he wanted to make it back before dark; there was a report to write. The horse attempted to head to the water trough, but he jerked on her bridle and pointed her in the direction of home.

A few miles from the tavern she became skittish. As he eased her up, he caught sight of a dark shape to his left. A black wolf. He looked to his right. Another. From the scabbard he pulled the loaded rifle, aiming at the first wolf. The animal had no fear; it looked directly back at him. Young Zahafian was right; it *was* like looking at the devil. He aimed for the bulk of the wolf's large body and squeezed the trigger, but nothing happened. He'd left the safety catch on. He cursed, released the catch, and raised the rifle again. But both wolves had disappeared.

Momentarily, Hamad considered going after them. Instead, he kicked the mare and cantered away. He would return with two of his men to hunt and destroy the whole pack. He felt both a rush of adrenaline and relief. He dug his heels harder into the mare's flanks and she broke into a gallop.

After a few more miles of hard riding, the mare's neck was streaked with sweat, but Hamad ignored this. He urged her on until he was absolutely sure he was safe.

Eventually, he allowed the horse to slow to a trot.

Before dismounting he looked around for a full five minutes. His mare drew deep, rasping breaths as her sweat-soaked flanks twitched.

Hamad needed to urinate. A combination of too much beer and the heavy riding had played havoc with his bladder. As he dismounted he reached for the rifle, but the mare bolted. Now on his backside, he looked after her and called her name. When he caught her, she would be punished. He stood, undid his flies, and relieved himself, head down, shoulders forward.

When he looked up, a large black wolf stood maybe five yards away smelling the air. Others joined it. One by one.

He counted six in total.

Basic training

I joined up when I was eighteen. There were one hundred and sixty of us. We got our number-one haircut, our mountain of kit, and before we could draw breath, we were lined up in four neat rows under the seven oak trees. Told to ball our fists, look left, raise our left arms straight out to the side, touch the shoulder of the man to the left of us and shuffle until we were exactly an arm's length apart. Four perfect rows of forty standing tall in front of the CO.

Colonel Izzard had seen action in the First Gulf War. He said we were following in the footsteps of men of honour. When the CO departed a sergeant told us we were nothing, dismissed us, and hounded us to our billets. The thirty-nine men either side of me would be my roommates for the next twenty-eight weeks. Each billet had its own corporal. We had the good fortune to get Corporal Couples. We were to call him Staff, nothing else. He was a little guy, a mixture of fitness and excess, a lifer, and a mean bastard. He strode into our billet and asked if there was anyone who was having second thoughts. If so, would they step forward? He waited a full minute. But no one stepped forward.

Then he gave us a speech of his own. We were not to lend money to anyone. If we did, we were up on a charge: there would be a restriction of privileges. We would call them RIPs. Being up on a charge could last for twenty-eight days. For less minor breaches of discipline there were press-ups. Corporal Couples told us that pain is a wonderful teacher.

He taught us how to bull our boots: light a tin of boot polish, blow it out, rub your cloth in the polish, and rub the polish in ever decreasing circles into the toe of the boot. After hours, days, weeks of this, the toe of the boot would shine like glass. He taught us how to make up our bunks to the correct army specification. How to iron our kit. All in regular lines. Corporal Couples taught us how to shave. He taught us how to shower. We stood in a semi-circle and watched while he showed us how much soap to use, how to lift our cocks and soap underneath.

Every morning a pissed-off junior officer and a ball-breaking sergeant looked for irregular lines, or dust and dirt; running their white-gloved fingers along door frames, behind radiators. Every day of those first few weeks the junior officer would lift his white-gloved index finger and speak with the sergeant. The sergeant would step forward and, depending on his mood, either demand press-ups or a show parade. Slowly, we began to learn. All except Birdagain.

Every morning Birdagain failed at something. There was shit on his beret, there was dirt on his boots, he hadn't shaved properly, his bed linen wasn't folded correctly. Corporal Couples would lean forward – his face an inch from Birdagain – and scream: Bird. AGAIN!

We all paid for it.

Corporal Couples was getting bollocked from the sergeant and he was passing it on to us. Birdagain thought it was funny. I tried to help him, and then I learnt something. The guy wasn't likeable – he was a self-centred bastard.

Doc was in the bunk next to mine. Doc was older, late twenties. He had a university degree. He just woke up one morning, said fuck it, and signed up. Doc said standards were slipping, fewer were signing up. He said the infantry needed more men for the war on terror. He told us Birdagain had been in and out of orphanages and short-term foster care all his life.

Doc said: All the army asks is that you follow simple instructions and show an aptitude for killing. If you can do that, you're part of the family.

It was six weeks before we got our hands on the SA8o. Corporal Couples told us: It is not a gun. It is a rifle! The Artillery use guns. The Infantry use rifles. Corporal Couples told us the SA8o was the most reliable weapon of its type in the world. Doc told me it was prone to gas stoppages in hot, dusty climates. I believed Doc.

Corporal Couples said any man who dropped his weapon or even let it out of his hands would be up on a charge. The SA8o would save our lives in combat. It was to be handled with care. Causing damage to a weapon was a step up from blasphemy. Birdagain pointed his weapon at his buddy and pulled the trigger. Firing an unloaded weapon causes damage to the firing pin. Birdagain was put on a charge. If Corporal Couples caught Birdagain doing the same thing again he would put his thumb in the firing mechanism, then his dick.

Halfway through our training it snowed. We woke up one morning and a white blanket covered everything. Doc said: They'll have a different torture for us today. After morning inspection and our visit to the slop jockeys, we were marched slipping and sliding, everyone out of step, to the lecture hall. Captain Ferdinand stood in front of a lectern and spoke. In a monotone voice he told us how to acclimatise to the heat and cold of the desert. During the day we were to take clothes off, according to the temperature, at night we were to put clothes on again, according to the temperature. He must have been short-sighted. We were all nodding off. My chin was dropping to my chest and then shooting up again. I looked around me. Every man sat in the lecture hall like a nodding dog while Captain Ferdinand told us how to warm up or cool down – the army way. Birdagain fell asleep.

Captain Ferdinand ordered us all out. If we were sleepy then the fresh air would wake us up. We stood for an hour in the snow. When we got back into the lecture hall we listened intently as Captain Ferdinand told us about the need to look after our feet by keeping them warm and dry. No one fell asleep.

Corporal Couples told us, if we made it to Iraq, there was something very important to add to our fifty pounds of kit: our NBC suits. NBC: Nuclear, Biological and Chemical. We all worried about Saddam. We had all seen the village of dead Kurds on CNN. Our NBC training involved walking into a wooden hut filled with CS gas wearing our suits; taking off our gas masks; answering: *name, rank, serial number* or any combination of the three in any order; putting our masks back on; blowing three times into the mask to clear it of gas; and answering the same question:

rank, serial number, name? Some panicked. Some masks were faulty. Doc said they did it deliberately. Those who failed would have to go back and do it again – vomiting, eyes streaming – until they got it right. Those who stepped out the wrong door would have to go back in.

We'd been there fourteen weeks and we were getting tight. We could square-bash all day without groin strain; our routines perfect. We could field strip our SA8os blindfolded, grease them, and reassemble them in under two minutes. We would pass morning inspections with ease – all of us, except Birdagain.

We needed a break from the shit. Taylor suggested we get a beer. Doc told us not to be fucking about; if we were caught, they'd throw us in the Glasshouse.

– One fucking beer is what I'm talking about.

– I'll have one, I said.

– Yeah, me too, said Birdagain.

Taylor looked at Birdagain.

– You wanna beer, you can fucking get them.

– I'll get them, I said. Bird'll fuck it up.

I walked to the NAAFI and bought four tins of Carlsberg. But one of the Monkeys spotted me. He shouted. I didn't stop. I made it back to the billet and hid the cans in the shower block. The Monkey came crashing in and told us to clear out our lockers.

We got an hour's sleep that night. There was to be a show parade in the morning in front of the CO. The culprit was to step forward. Taylor said they'd kick me out, running from an MP like that. Doc said too many men had been invalided out already. The army needed men. He said there was only one way out of it: They'll kick one out, but they won't kick four out.

The four of us would step forward. It was agreed.

The next morning we stood in the square in front of the CO. He gave a speech about the regiment's code of honour and how a lack of discipline can cost lives. Doc, Taylor, and I stepped forward. Birdagain stood stock-still.

They marched us double-time to the Glasshouse. Doc scrubbed floors with a toothbrush. I was detailed to shovel snow with Taylor. When they couldn't find any more paths to clear they made us dig holes, then fill them in again. I thought I preferred it to the tooth-brushing. I was fit back then, but it didn't matter. They took me beyond that. My hands were blistered and had swollen so much I couldn't put my gloves back on, but what kept me going was my hatred for Birdagain. I knew Taylor was the same.

They kept us for two days, beasting us; screaming in our faces, kicking and punching us, pissing in our tea. Taylor told the Monkeys it tasted better than the bromide. Taylor was the toughest guy in the unit; he could bench press two-ten in multiple reps. Before the Glasshouse, he carried our company flag, and our general-purpose machine gun – the Jimpy. And *he* was struggling. He took sick; his face was the colour of a ripe tomato. But the Monkeys didn't care; they laughed at him and called him the Ribena Man. I felt like I was about ready to just lie down and give up. I hoped that Taylor would get so sick, or even die, that they would have to leave me alone. After forty-eight hours without sleep they marched us double-time back to our billet. The rest of the boys helped with our kit and hauled us out of bed before morning inspection.

But that wasn't the end of it: there were R.I.P.s for the three of us. For the next twenty-eight days, while the rest of the troop cleaned their kit, we would be given a detail. We would sweep the parade square of snow and leaves, an impossible task. None of us spoke to Birdagain. Taylor wanted to kill him.

Then, one night, towards the end of our training, Birdagain came over and said: No one's speaking to me.

I couldn't look at him. I couldn't say anything.

– I wanted to step forward, but I just couldn't, he said.

All my hatred for Corporal Couples, for the CO, for the sergeant, for the MPs, was nothing compared to my hatred for Birdagain.

– Why did you run? he said. You should have stopped for the MP.

Something broke within me. I tackled him right across the room and on to his bunk and tried to hit him, but he was on top of me. Then Taylor and Doc stepped in. Others got up off their bunks. Every man in the room took part. Birdagain fought and screamed and spat and cried. We stuffed the cloth he used for bulling his boots into his mouth and we beat him, and we kept beating him, until he stopped fighting back, and we boot-polished him with the cloths we used to bull our own boots. Every inch of his body was covered. We took our time.

When we had finished, we carried him down to the shower block. There were two baths down there that we used for cleaning our kit. We filled one with cold water and threw him in. When we got back to the billet no one was laughing. We had done the right thing, but it didn't feel right. We all sat down on the lip of our bunks and silently cleaned our kit. I don't know how long went by, maybe half an hour, but there was no sign of Birdagain.

I walked down the corridor, opened the door a little,

and looked in. The water was black, there was a line of scum on the white enamel of the bath, and he just lay there looking at the ceiling.

– Bird, up to fuck! I said.

He didn't answer. I ran back to the billet and told the boys. Taylor hauled him out and performed cardiac compressions. His hands kept slipping from Birdagain's chest. Black water came up out of Birdagain's lungs, spewing from his mouth and onto the tiled floor, and I thought for a minute that we were saved. But he was dead. We all knew the enormity of it. We just stood there for what seemed like forever.

– Fuck it. Let's clean him up, said Doc.

We drained the bath, cleaned the scum off it, and wiped the place down. Then we filled the bath with warm water and cleaned Birdagain in the regulation manner. He was the cleanest he'd ever been.

– There'll be an inquiry, said Doc. This is how we found him. *Agreed!*

We all agreed.

Corporal Couples called for the MO. The MO examined Birdagain, and he looked at us like he knew. When Colonel Izzard arrived the MO said there was probably some underlying pre-existing medical condition. There was no inquiry; Bird had no family.

At the Passing Out, we lined up under the seven oaks for the last time.

Colonel Izzard walked along the ranks, shook our hands, and told us to always honour the regiment.

When I finally got to the desert, I was ready to kill again.

Latin, Olde English, Celtic, and horseshit

Following a tidal surge, it washed up in the back garden of old Mrs Doherty's beach cottage. Old Mrs Doherty had been dead for years. This thing was alive.

It was young Declan Moone who found it. At first, he thought it was a whale. But it had no tail and whales don't have legs. He walked around to the front of the great hoary mass and it raised its colossal head. On each milky eye was a white sucker with white frills. He looked out to sea, then ran up Main Street to Quinn's public house.

A crowd followed Declan Moone back down Main Street to old Mrs Doherty's; their nosiness overriding their skepticism. When they arrived, the great grey beast was still there, sleeping. The pub owner, Eddie Quinn, said they should build a fence immediately to stop it escaping back into the sea. Seamus McSheffrey, who worked for the council, said they would need the council digger.

Someone said: You'll need council approval for that.

– Fuck that, someone else said. It'll be a fossil by then.

It was agreed that Seamus McSheffrey should get the digger at once.

A fence was built; an extremely good and sturdy one, considering the short time involved. People of the town who had never joined in with anything joined in with the building of the fence, for they saw the possibilities.

When the structure was completed it was already dark. By now the entire village stood in the back garden.

Adie McDaid, who had once studied in Derry, and was always on the internet, said: We need to keep the thing wet, like they do with beached whales.

The back door of old Mrs Doherty's cottage was kicked in, buckets appeared, and a line of people poured water over the creature, until the ground became sodden.

Eddie-the-publican said they would need a plan. The town solicitor, Trevor Buchanan, stepped forward and said they would need to lay claim to it legally before the press were informed.

Everyone followed the two men back up Main

Street to the bar.

On the walk up, Eddie-the-publican and Trevor-the-solicitor remained, heads lowered, in vital conversation.

When the crowd arrived at the bar, everyone wanted a drink; even the members of the local Alcoholics Anonymous group.

– We'll build a museum.

– You mean a zoo?

– A theme park.

– Ten euros entrance.

– Twenty!

– Make them pay in sterling.

– There'll be Americans.

– We can sell all sorts of shit!

In between serving pints, Eddie-the-publican took down the miniature framed blackboard (for tourists) that always sat above the till and, with a wet finger, rubbed out the generous 1.20 exchange rate. In its place he wrote 1.10. Then, before setting it back above the till, he wet his finger again, and rubbed out the smiley face that was always chalked underneath. And smiled.

– It's the property of the town, said Eddie-the-publican, turning to face the crowd. Am I right?

– It was me who found it, said young Declan

Moone. It's mine.

– It was found on old Mrs Doherty's land.

Trevor-the-solicitor, a tall lean man, who was in permanent need of a haircut, and always – even on a Saturday – wore the same dark blue suit, stepped forward.

– The deeds to old Mrs Doherty's house have lapsed. In effect the garden is *Bona vacantia*.

He continued talking, and the longer he talked the more he himself lapsed, moving easily into a peculiar Donegal legalese until, eventually, no one could understand a single word he said. It was a fresh hybrid of Latin, Olde English, Celtic and horseshit.

Eddie-the-publican raised a hand.

– Okay, Trevor, thank you... thank you.

He addressed young Declan Moone.

– As the finder of the beast there'll be an upfront payment made to yourself.

And he set him up a pint of Heineken, on the house, like.

– Who's looking after it now? asked someone.

Everyone looked at each other. The younger ones were the quickest to the door. And, in a rush – like that of a marathon just commenced – they ran from the pub, down Main Street, to the back garden.

The thing was still there, and still alive. It had moved

onto its back now. And was snoring. As it snored, its huge whiskered mouth wobbled.

When Eddie-the-publican finally caught up, and caught his breath, he said: We'll need two people to do two hour shifts through the night until daylight. There'll be chairs and quilts brought down.

The crowd dropped their heads and shuffled their feet in the soaked grass.

– And I'll provide the drink, he said.

– I can do the first shift, shouted Joe Braiden, who received disability and worked as a coalman.

– Me too, said Paul Macken, the plasterer.

– Agreed.

They all hurried back to the bar.

*

The next morning, at first light, Anthony-the-postman, who never slept late, even when drunk, woke Eddie-the-publican.

He got up slowly, stepped over the bodies, and rubbed his eyes.

– Whose shift is it? he said, automatically.

Heads lifted; farts, groans, and coughs filled the bar. Again, the crowd poured out of the bar en masse, and ran down Main Street; this time, more in the manner of those finishing a marathon.

When they got to old Mrs Doherty's back garden,

Sean-Patrick-the-car-mechanic and Julie, who worked part-time in the Centra, were asleep together on a comfy chair. The beast had gone. From the outside, the sturdy fence had been crushed. Something had come to get it. Its mother?

Each member of the village made their way home in solitary hungover silence.

When Eddie-the-publican returned to the public house the place was a bombsite. The floor was awash with beer, there were muddy footprints on the bar counter, and the shelves behind the bar were bare. He walked behind the counter and boiled the kettle. While he waited, he took down the little blackboard that sat above the till and rubbed out the 1.10 he had written only hours before. In its place he wrote 1.20. Then, before placing it back above the till, he drew a smiley face. And frowned.

In the absence
of a father

The girl said it was a green car. My Uncle Gene didn't drive a green car; he drove a van, and if you saw it you wouldn't forget it. It was a big red one with flames shooting up from the wheel arches, and on each of the mud flaps was a little Dixie flag.

Of course, he could have borrowed a green car. I asked him about that, and he said: I wouldn't drive a green car if you paid me.

The girl also said the man was wearing a white shirt.

Uncle Gene said: When did you ever see me wearing a white shirt? He didn't even wear one in court.

Uncle Gene wore his full head of dirty-blond hair greased back and set in a quiff. He had tattoos running right around his forearms; dark-green and red, with the scales of dragons and nautical stars. They ran right the way to the end of his wrists where they stopped suddenly. In the summer, when he came over to sunbathe at my mother's house, I saw the writing on his back and chest – lyrics from songs I didn't know.

The girl was sixteen. She didn't tell her parents about it until the next day. She said the man had threatened to kill her if she breathed a word. She also said the man knew where she lived.

I was more like my Uncle Gene than my mother in looks, personality, everything – in that strange way that genes pass on sometimes. My mom said he was the black sheep of the family; when they were children he was always getting into trouble. She remembered he'd been expelled from school, but she couldn't remember exactly what for.

Mom said: when he was young, he could have had any girl he wanted, but he was more interested in cars and motorbikes.

At school he was regarded as stupid. The truth is he was dyslexic, but he was smart, one of the smartest people I knew.

Each summer we would rent a house on the shore and sometimes Uncle Gene would babysit. When mom went out, I could sit up late and watch Robert De Niro videos. Uncle Gene was an expert.

– What was his name in *King of Comedy*?
– Rupert Pupkin.
– In *Mean Streets*?

– Johnny Boy.

– *The Godfather*?

– Don Corleone. Real name... Vito Andolini.

– *Taxi Driver*?

– Travis Bickle.

He would act out scenes.

– You talkin' to me?... You talkin' to me?... Well, I'm the only one standin' here...

He drank bottles of Michelob and smoked skinny roll-ups. I took out the empties and hid them under household garbage so mom wouldn't see them. When she came back home after a night out, I'd be in bed and Uncle Gene would be asleep on the sofa. In the absence of a father he helped shape me. I owed him a lot.

The summer before the thing happened with the girl, mom said I was too big for a babysitter. Uncle Gene fell out with her over that. He spent that summer with my Great-Aunt Margaret in Vancouver.

When he came back, he had fancy license plates for his van and a red dress for me. He must have asked mom my dress size – it fitted perfectly.

When the crime was committed, I was sixteen, the same age as the girl.

The girl said the man had chased her. The lawyer argued that Uncle Gene was incapable of chasing anyone; there was medical evidence. He was born with scoliosis. The curvature in his spine was such that he was incapable of running any distance.

Uncle Gene was given six years.

I wrote him and he wrote me back.

He served four years of that sentence.

The week before his release, he phoned and asked if I could pick him up.

I said: Of course.

On the day of his release he said: Come after lunch.

He'd been waiting four years to get out and he wouldn't be processed till after lunch.

At two o'clock, I got a message from him saying he'd be ready in an hour.

On the drive there I felt an excitement I hadn't felt since I was a little girl.

He stood alone in the parking lot in rolled up jeans, cowboy boots, and a tight denim jacket. There was an old duffel bag at his feet, and he was smoking a skinny roll-up. He'd changed. His hair was graying, and he'd put on some weight.

He walked over to the car. When he walked, he hardly lifted either foot off the ground. It was like he glided. He hugged me, lifted me right off my feet. I could smell soap and cigarettes, and I wanted to tell him about the times he'd led me by the hand along the beach, watched De Niro films with me, took me for rides in his van, but I couldn't say a thing, I was crying.

He opened the back door of the car and threw his duffel bag on the back seat. Then he got in.

I pulled out of the parking lot and drove.

– Where do you want to go first? I asked.

– I want an ice cream.

– Dairy Queen?

– Dairy Queen is good.

He asked how mom was. I told him she was good. He flicked his roll-up out of the passenger window. I didn't know what to say. He kept talking. I kept driving, looking for a Dairy Queen.

Pain relief

I t's dangerous for my wife to be bored. I know this from experience.

She steps out of the way as the ER nurse moves in to inject the vein in my left arm.

Immediately, the world is the way I'd always imagined it should be.

A porter wheels in a gas canister – a big silver scuba tank.

– Thanks, I say.

– No problem, he says. Enjoy.

The nurse attaches a long clear line to the tank, clips the other end of the clear line to a mask, then fits me with the mask.

– Just gentle breaths, she says, turning the valve on the tank clockwise.

When the doctor arrives, he lifts my hand by the wrist and examines it.

The more I suck on the gas the younger he gets.

When he first arrived, just minutes ago, he was middle-aged, now he's early twenties.

As he scrutinizes my hand, I can see the sweat in small beads on his top lip.

From my position, the hand – with the steak knife through it – looks like one of those joke shop tricks.

The doctor looks to the nurse.

– We need to call a surgeon.

My wife checks her watch.

– Just pull it out, I say, from behind my mask. It doesn't hurt.

– It doesn't hurt because you're on morphine and gas, says the nurse.

– The problem is I don't know if the blade's touching a blood vessel, says the doctor. There's a lot of blood.

– Yeah, says my wife. He bleeds a lot.

– You mean—

– No, I just mean he bleeds a lot.

A high-pitched alarm sounds on one of the machines.

Everybody stops.

The doctor looks to the nurse.

She bends over, close to my ear.

– Take it easy on the gas, she says. Slowly... slowly... just little breaths.

I eyeball her and continue sucking it in.

The doctor whispers to my wife: This is serious.

I can hear him clearly. I can hear for miles.

He continues examining the hand as a child might examine a ladybird.

- We may have to amputate.
- Well, says my wife. He has another one.

F is for fish

My landline is ringing. I wonder if it's Simon. Simon has been my sponsor for the past two years. Like me he's an alcoholic; but Simon is in recovery.

He gave me his two goldfish to look after while he's on holiday. He thinks this little act will keep me sober. He's wrong. Before Simon gave me his goldfish, I knew I was going to drink. The compulsion for alcohol had returned.

I try to move but nothing happens.

When the phone stops ringing, I hear music. Shauna is home; she lives in the flat directly below. She looks different every time I see her. Sometimes, I walk by her on the stairs, say hello, and don't immediately realise it's her. She has that chameleon-like quality that great method actors have. She should have gone to Hollywood. Instead, she's trapped in a flat, mixing antipsychotics with class As. She'll put on a track and play it over and over again. Today it's Nena's '99 Red Balloons' – the German version. Shauna is stuck somewhere in the mid-eighties, when she was a child and life held no fears.

It seems things can't get any worse, but I've had rock bottoms before. Rocks bottoms alone are not enough to make me quit. I need to change inside. Simon talks about the jumping-off point, the time when he decided he'd had enough. It was a rock bottom connected to a psychic change.

Simon says I should move a muscle when I'm in mental pain: *Move a muscle, change a thought*. But I can't move. I'm paralysed.

I'll play I Spy.

I Spy with my little eye something beginning with A.

This is an easy one. A is for Alcohol. There are four empty vodka bottles on the dresser.

I read recently that more people drown in the desert than die of thirst. Flash floods are the killer. It doesn't rain for a long time. When it does rain, people aren't expecting it, and it really rains, and people just drown. That's what it's like when I drink, a flash flood.

I return to I Spy.

I can't see anything beginning with B, but I think I might die of boredom. Sherlock Holmes took morphine to stave off boredom. Maybe a modern-day Sherlock Holmes will look around my bedroom, and as '99 Red Balloons' ascends from below, he'll deduce: All is not as it appears, Watson. Something hastened his demise.

– What do you mean, Holmes?

– '99 Red Balloons', my dear Dr Watson!

– You weren't bored again this morning, were you, Holmes?

C is for crack.

No, not the drug; I'm talking about the cracks in the ceiling. I'm sure I've noticed the big cracks, but I didn't notice the little ones until now. I suppose if you look closely at anything for long enough, you'll see the little cracks.

I used to think I was a born survivor, one of those people you read about in *Reader's Digest* who gnaw their own legs off in a snowstorm, then slide a hundred miles on their arse to the nearest hospital and now they have a new career as a skiing instructor. And maybe I was a survivor at one time, but not anymore.

D is for dehydration.

That would be a good one for my mother. When her friends ask over the garden fence with clasped hands what I died of, she'll be able to say: He died of thirst.

– Oh, was he an adventurer?

– Sort of.

The phone rings again; I'll bet it's Simon.

When I wake it's the late afternoon of my second day. The peculiar thing about my present situation is that, although I'm paralysed by the effect of an alcoholic binge, I'm perfectly rational. Despite this rationality, there's acceptance, or denial: instead of worrying about myself I'm worried about Simon's two goldfish. I can't remember when I last fed them. I'm quite sure I fed them for the first day or two, but I think I may have added the whole container of fish food sometime in the middle of the binge.

Again, I fall asleep worrying about them.

And I dream.

In the dream there are two huge, bloated, white-eyed goldfish floating on their sides at the top of a small glass tank.

When I wake, my jaw and tongue are sore.

E is for electric shock.

My muscles are in spasm, my buttocks, thighs, calves, biceps, and stomach all cramp up and release. When the spasms are over, I'm exhausted, but I find I can move. I turn onto my side and manage to get myself semi-upright at the side of the bed. I'm still wearing my clothes, even my shoes. On the floor is a bag containing broken glass from a vodka bottle I dragged up the stairs to my flat, days earlier.

I make it towards the kitchen. There's a long mirror in the landing, framed in gold. I stop to look at myself. But it's not me; it's an intruder, a bearded skeleton who has ransacked my flat.

I make it to the kitchen tap and quench my thirst.

Then I reach to the cupboard above the kettle for a chill pill. Diazepam will give me a soft landing, but it's also a muscle relaxant. The tablets are in one of those little bottles that have a safety cap to stop kids opening them. My brain tells my hand to squeeze the lid while turning, but somewhere along the line my hand doesn't receive the signal. A task that would take me seconds now takes minutes. This is how it will be for the next few days. On the bottle it says: *Take one as required*. I take four and, in a couple of hours, I will take another four.

I return to the kitchen sink, sipping water from the palm of my hand, but my head is still in the bedroom. I know I have forgotten something important.

And then I remember... F is for fish.

The true language
of primates

Harper sits under the shade of a flat-topped acacia tree smoking a Marlboro. His clothes are filthy, his face is tight from the sun, and he feels completely and utterly at home.

It's his final day in Africa: his PhD is complete – it's been ready for weeks – he's stalling, and he knows it.

Moses, the Head Ranger, hands him a mug of strong black coffee. He looks up at his friend and thanks him with a smile.

Harper scans the baboon troop, until he finds Gimli. The youngster is chasing grasshoppers; snatching them acrobatically from the angled sunlight. Harper remembers the day he was born. He has an affinity with this young baboon.

He sips the bitter coffee. This time tomorrow he'll be with Julia in London. They've agreed to marry when he receives his doctorate. That's the arrangement. So, he'll return to skinny lattes, cars, money;

a life in which people hurtle from one place to another. A life in which there are so many words, yet so little understanding. Now he's not sure if he speaks her language.

He understands baboon language, and that knowledge has saved his life. A year previous, Gimli screeched the warning for snake directly at him as he would to another troop member. Two feet in front of Harper, perfectly camouflaged, was a coiled Gaboon viper. He would never have seen the snake without Gimli's warning.

He looks over at the troop again until he spots the youngster.

– You'll miss your flight, says Moses.

Harper rubs his sole in the dry dirt.

– I know, Moses, he says.

Calls to
distant places

It was two in the morning. When I got out of the taxi, I saw my neighbour, Reg, across the street standing at his front gate. I hadn't spoken to him in months; his wife had cancer and my wife had just had a baby.

– Hi Reg, I said.

He motioned to me.

– What's up? I said.

– It's Bruno.

Bruno was Reg's golden retriever.

– I came downstairs for a cigarette, it must have been his heart, he's been on medication.

I didn't know what to say.

– I need to get him in the boot of the car. I don't want Grace to see him. She's been through enough already.

We walked together up the slope of the driveway to the house. He opened the car boot and lifted out his fishing gear. There was a chill and I could see my own breath.

Reg came out of the garage with black bin liners and arranged them carefully along the bottom of the boot. When he had finished, I followed him into the house. I hadn't been in the house since last summer. When we walked inside, I could smell synthetic air freshener.

In the living room, the dog was lying on a throw on the sofa.

Reg had really let the place go: on one of the seats, beside the television, was a pile of old magazines and newspapers. There were ashes and white tissues in the grate and on the hearth.

Reg got on his knees and cradled Bruno's head and I tried to lift his hind legs. He was still warm.

Then Reg said: Wait. He placed the throw over him, and we lifted him off the sofa in that manner. We carried him carefully through each doorway to the outside and placed him in the boot of the car. Then Reg bent down and kissed him on the forehead before finally closing the boot. I patted Reg on the shoulder and we both went back inside.

In the kitchen he reached up above the grill, opened a cupboard, and took out a bottle of Bushmills. Then he nodded towards the sink: Help yourself to a glass.

As I walked towards the sink, I kicked a bowl of dried dog food. It was half empty. And I cursed.

– Sorry about the mess, said Reg.

I lifted a glass and rinsed it under the hot tap, running my fingers inside and along the rim to clean it.

I'd been drinking beer all night and I wasn't ready for the whiskey. It tasted earthy. It would take a bit of getting used to. I patted my pockets for my cigarettes, stood up, and offered one to Reg.

– I'm just going to check on Grace, he said. I'm not smoking in the house anymore.

I heard his weight on the stairs as I patted every pocket for my lighter. When I found it, I stepped outside onto the patio. The intruder light came on immediately.

I remembered last summer. We had only just moved in. Reg had called at the door to introduce himself. He had caught two sea trout. The male fish was around four pounds, the female a pound lighter.

He brought me over a generous cut from each fish. My wife, Anna, said she couldn't eat them after having just seen them whole. I wrapped them in tinfoil and cooked them in the oven with just a little olive oil, salt, and pepper. They didn't taste like farmed fish. These fish, you could taste the river in them.

Anna said we should invite Reg and Grace over for a drink. They both came over with wine and beer. And, when the sun moved behind our house, we all carried our drinks across the street to Reg and Grace's. I remembered Grace carrying her sandals in one hand and a wine glass in the other.

They were both older than us by twenty years but there was a bond. Grace really hit it off with Anna. I think in many ways they were similar – they had a lot in common.

Reg had said he would take me fly fishing He gave me a cork-handled beginner's rod, showed me how to cast. I had been practising with that rod; casting from my patio until I could land the fly on my compost bin. The fishing season had come and gone – I'd paid £120 for a fishing licence – and I hadn't got to fish.

Reg stepped outside. The intruder light came back on.

– She's sleeping, he said.

I offered him a cigarette and he accepted. Stood there in a white short-sleeved shirt, he didn't seem to notice the cold.

– How's Anna?

– She's good, I said. Anna's good.

– And the baby?

– The baby's good.

– A good sleeper?

I nodded. The truth is I was sleeping in the spare room. I felt like Anna and I were drifting apart since the baby had come along.

– My son left before you moved in, said Reg. He's an accountant, lives in Australia now.

He drained the glass.

– I might visit when things settle down here.

He went back inside for the bottle and, when he came back outside, he asked: Have you changed a nappy yet?

– Not yet, I said.

– I never changed a single nappy. Grace did it all.

Then he drained the glass, looked up at the sky.

– It's my turn now, he said.

I lifted the glass, but I didn't drink from it.

– Reg, I said. I gotta go.

I offered him my hand. He shook it.

– Tell Anna I said hello, he said. And say hi to the baby.

Then he walked me through the house. On the front porch he hugged me, and he didn't let go.

– I'm sorry about the fishing, he said.

Who won the
donkey derby?

I open the door of the bar and stop momentarily to allow my eyes to adjust to the change in light. There are only two small windows, and they're low set, so that even early in the day it's dim inside.

Biddy Barr, the owner, sits behind the counter on a stool. The bar was once the living room and back room of her family house.

There's only one other punter. He sits on a stool at the far end of the counter; his back to the television and the fire, with two pints of Smithwick's in front of him.

It's early. Already, he looks drunk.

– Who won the donkey derby? he says, to no one in particular.

The small red tractor outside, with the hand-painted number plate and the cushion inside the plastic Centra carrier bag on the seat, is his.

His name's Magill, Ger Magill.

He drives that small red tractor into town like you'd take your car, and he owns farmland up at Quigley's Point. But he doesn't farm the land – something happened to him when he was a child. He drinks.

Biddy gets up off her stool.

– A pint of Heineken, is it?

– Yes, please.

I lean forward and watch her pouring. As I lean over the counter, I can see into the kitchen. It's like the kitchen of any house in the town. There's a combined food and water bowl for her cat on the linoleum floor.

– Who won the donkey derby? says Ger Magill.

– What's it like out? asks Biddy.

I have to think. I look down at the counter.

– It's dry, I say, finally.

She raises her chin.

– That's a blessing.

Biddy isn't one for conversation. She isn't one for anything really, but there are no snide remarks if you suddenly show up after months spent drinking up the town.

I take a gulp of Heineken and pull a face.

– Do ya want a wee splash of lemonade?

I blow out. And nod.

Biddy unscrews the lid on a glass bottle of brown lemonade that sits in amongst the other glass bottles of cordial on a circular tray. And she pours a splash of brown lemonade into what remains of the white head of the Heineken.

It goes down a bit easier with the hint of lemonade. I finish it quickly. Then I let out a sigh.

Biddy takes the empty glass from my hand and angles it under the pump. With Biddy you only have to tip your empty glass forward and she'll rise from her stool, take the glass from your hand, and refill it.

– Who won the donkey derby? says Ger Magill.

I stare in his direction, then at the television behind him, but I can't decipher a thing.

When Biddy sets the second pint in front of me it looks much better than the first.

– D'ya want another wee splash of lemonade?

– No thanks, I'll just go with it.

– Right you are.

This one goes down easier.

When I'm on my third pint, Ger Magill gets up off his stool and walks slowly, in a stoop, from the far end of the bar to where I'm sitting.

He looks directly at me.

– D'ya hear me... who won the donkey derby?

I don't know the man. I mean, I know of him. I know his father was a drunk, and a mean bastard. And I've been stuck behind that red tractor often enough.

– I don't know, I say. Who won the donkey derby?

He stabs his thumb into his chest.

– Me! he says.

Sunbeams and the Almighty

Before sitting on the barber's chair I take off my coat and hang it on the coat stand.

– And what can I do for you, sir?

– Take it all off, please.

– To number one, sir?

– Please.

Earlier this morning, following a good night's sleep – a rare event – I'd made two decisions. The first decision was the haircut.

I like coming to the barber's, and it's a long time since I've been.

The barber bends at the knees, raises his hands each side of my head, framing it, looking at me in the mirror.

– Would you like the hair washed, sir?

I wonder how much extra that'll cost.

– Yes. Thank you.

He extends his palm to the sink.

I get up, walk to another black leather chair, sit down and rest the back of my neck against cold porcelain.

When he turns on the water, he tests it with his hand then showers my scalp. But the water temperature isn't right. It's too hot. Then too cold.

By the time he's finished I feel overcome by something.

When I open my eyes, the light is different: brighter, richer.

I get up again, much slower this time, and walk to the chair I'd sat in originally.

The light is most definitely different. Everything's different. There's a metallic taste in my mouth.

The second decision I'd made earlier that morning was to stop taking my medication.

As I sit in the chair, I look in the mirror.

On the wooden bench behind me are five people. I recognise the faces from different periods of my life.

– Day off?

– What?

The barber runs the buzzer upwards then sideways along the right side of my head, before stopping and flicking his wrist to allow the cut hair to drop to the floor.

– Is it your day off work?

– Yes, it's my day off.

– It's turned colder. Have you any holidays planned?

– Can I ask you a question?

– Fire away.

– Are you busy today?

– Not particularly.

– I mean... right now... are you busy?

– What do you have in mind?

– How can I put this... is there anyone else in the shop?

The barber stops cutting and takes a single step back, buzzer in his right hand, still buzzing.

– Hey... what is this?

– I don't mean anything; I was just wondering if the people I see in the mirror are real.

– What people?

– Then they're not real.

– Listen, friend, I'm going to have to ask you to leave.

– Okay, it's not a problem.

I stand up, reach into my jeans' pocket.

– Forget about it, he says. It's on the house.

– I'll pay four-fifty for half a cut.

– Three will do, it's more like a third.

When I get home, I look in the bathroom mirror; my head is shaved to the scalp on the right-hand side; the remainder of my hair overgrown.

I walk into the kitchen, open the cabinet above the kettle, and take out my medication. Then I boil the kettle for a cup of tea.

It's no big deal, in a week or two it'll grow out.

The god of this world

I believe I met the devil, and I know he saved my life. You may think I'm crazy, but I know what happened, I was there.

Three days before Christmas they flew us in. Our job was to secure a compound on the edge of the world. It was a police station – or at least it had been. The previous occupants were lined up at the entrance, on the hardpacked earth, and beheaded one by one. The village stood and watched, they had no choice.

The day after we flew in, a mortar crew appeared. The old man who led the crew was experienced; he never appeared in the same place twice, and he never came within range of our M16s. We'd scope them, and fire off a few rounds, but they were safe, and they knew it.

The mortar was an old M2 muzzle-loading smooth-bore. It wasn't accurate but we knew they only had to get lucky once. Our lieutenant called in Hellfire, but the mortar crew never stayed longer than twenty minutes; by the time Air Support arrived they'd gone.

Then, on Christmas Eve, he arrived out of the sky during a hailstorm. I didn't see him get out of the chopper, but I did see LTV walk off the flat roof to greet him. LTV was our squad leader – we called him LTV or Lieutenant V – his real name was Vincent.

On each section of the flat roof there were two of us at all times. We buddied up. I shared the east side with Lucerne. He was a preacher's son; I didn't share his beliefs, but I trusted him with my life.

When the lieutenant came back up onto the roof, he said to us: I have a surprise for you.

– I hope it's Santa.

– Even better than Santa.

– What's better than Santa?

– A sniper.

– We both shut up.

Later that day I got a good look at him; he was tall and slim, in a black turban – a Patka – worn in the style of the local tribesmen; the long tail of cloth hanging down his back, but he was no tribesman. The remainder of his kit was an assortment of army issue: wrap-around goggles, desert combats, and boots the Danes favored.

He walked across the roof and glanced in our direction, but he didn't greet us; he was taking it all in. Under the shade of an olive tarp he lay down, surveying the terrain, setting his ammunition in the sun. I'd seen snipers do this before; warming the rounds to give them better distance. From where I sat, I could see he was using lightweight 7.62mm rounds. Then he set up the Dragunov, doping the scope on the rifle, making miniature adjustments. I knew these rifles had a range of around one thousand yards when used with these lightweight rounds, but the mortar crew hadn't come closer than one mile.

When Lucerne saw the Dragunov and the ammunition, I knew he thought the same as me: he could never make the shot. He took out his miniature blue Bible, held it close to his eyes, and began reading Scripture aloud. My nerves were frayed, and I wanted to tell Lucerne to knock it off, but I was scared. I didn't believe in God, but I didn't believe in dying either.

The sniper lay listening to the Scripture. And, although I could only see his eyes, I believe he was smiling.

Later that afternoon he took off his large desert goggles and shouted to me: Get the lieutenant!

Without those goggles I saw that his face had been horribly burned. When he removed the black cloth from his mouth he had no lips, and I saw his long yellow teeth, right down to the bare gums.

Lucerne ran down the stone steps to get the lieutenant.

A white Hilux appeared and the crew of three got out to set up the mortar.

At the same time, a spotter on a motorbike rode up from the east to co-ordinate everything by mobile phone. The spotter was a big man. We watched him arrive, the little motorbike wobbling on the uneven ground beneath his huge weight.

I could hear LTV spotting for the sniper.

– Two o'clock... eighteen hundred yards... zero wind...

An older, bearded man, a mobile phone in one hand, a pair of heavy binoculars in the other, led the mortar crew. Immediately, we heard the familiar shump. I tensed, listening to hear where it might land.

It was long.

I wanted to shout at the sniper to take the fucking shot.

He fired.

– Miss... six yards right... six yards high.

I scoped the mortar crew. They seemed to sense something, but they continued.

He chambered another round.

Another shot.

I had my eye to my rifle scope. A full two seconds from the sound of the shot I saw one of the mortar crew fall backwards.

– Hit!

He fired again. This time the old man dropped while still holding his phone and binoculars.

– Hit!

I looked to the spotter; he was on his motorbike, disappearing as fast as he could, bouncing up and down on the uneven trail.

The sniper picked up the Dragunov and strode to the east.

Seconds later a round struck the spotter, pitching him forward. The motorbike lay on its side, the rear wheel spinning sand, then continuing to spin.

He walked back to the tarp.

The remaining man from the mortar crew had turned the pickup in a wide circle. The high pitch of the engine carried along the flat desert plain. It was revving too high, and I thought: he can't drive: he's too young.

That final shot, I didn't look.

Lucerne told me it was the most incredible thing he'd ever seen. Through his scope he saw a pink mist, then he watched as the headless driver continued along the road in the pickup. He said it was supernatural, and then he said: I do believe that sniper is the Antichrist.

On Christmas morning, the sniper sat down below

with his rifle across his lap, waiting to be picked up by the bird.

Lucerne saw me watching him. He asked if, for once, I'd like to join him in prayer.

I nodded.

Side by side, we knelt down on that roof and silently prayed.

But I doubt we were praying to the same thing.

Plastic Jesus

Floors lay on the sofa, taking the occasional hit off the pipe. He looked out through the fly screen, idly hooked on whatever caught his eye. Directly across the street a little kid was riding his tricycle in a small backyard. Floors knew the kid's parents; the father worked in construction, the mother waitressed at the Sunrise Diner. The parents were around the same age as himself, and good people, but the house was right on the Amtrak line. It was no place for a kid to play.

He inhaled deeply from the pipe and held it, watching the kid across the street moving in ever-tighter circles. And, when the Southwestern Chief roared past, he was so high he thought it was a fucking earthquake.

He must have fallen asleep after that. When he woke, the sun was just going down. He looked outside and saw a big ball of moon in the sky. It was huge and bright, but the sun hadn't yet fallen. It just didn't seem right to him, the sun and moon both together.

He was still lying on the sofa wondering if it meant anything, the sun and moon together like that, when Crow arrived back.

– I was calling you to come get me. I had to pay ten bucks for a cab.

– I fell asleep, said Floors.

– Where's my fuckin' pipe, man?

– It's on the table in front of you.

The pipe was a real work of art: all carved animal and Indian heads, and it had two little wheels on the bottom so you could roll it over to your smoking buddy. Crow lifted a bag of grass from the table, nipped off little bits of green and orange-tinged bud with the nails of his thumb and forefinger, and filled up the bowl of the pipe. Then he lit it with a yellow disposable lighter, set his lips on the end of the pipe, and drew a deep breath. He had something on his mind.

– How much you owe me?

Floors continued lying on the sofa looking at the ceiling.

– Three months on the rent.

– That's twelve hundred, right? said Crow.

Floors moved his chin up and down.

– You take me to Austin and back, I'll forget about the rent and throw in an extra twelve hundred.

Floors sat up. He didn't even need to think about it, he said he'd do it.

– It's a fifty hour round trip. No stopping.

– Okay, said Floors.

– Just one thing, said Crow. You gotta stay clean for the trip. Drink as much coffee as you want, but that's it.

– Okay, said Floors again, and then he asked: What's in Austin?

– Business.

Two days later, Crow got up before lunch and made a phone call, then he walked into Floors' room and said: We're going today?

Floors said: Yeah... sure.

He packed a change of socks and a warm coat, then walked to the bathroom for his toothbrush. When he walked past Crow's room, he saw him wrap a denim shirt around his .38 snub-nose and push it deep into his green duffel bag.

An hour later, Floors was driving his big Dodge Ram out of town. Once he got on the interstate, he put his foot on the gas. The drive was all straight road with nothing to see but paddle cactus, shredded tires, and roadkill.

Sometimes, Floors would edge over the speed limit, and Crow would lean in from the back and say: Easy on the speed.

They were somewhere in the high desert when Floors said: I gotta take a piss.

– Yeah, me too, said Crow. Pull over.

When Floors got out, something ran from the other side of the road, under the van, and out the other side. Without even thinking, Floors ran after it. It went down the side of a steep embankment toward a dry riverbed and Floors slid down on his ass after it. When he caught up with it, it just rolled into a ball. It was a baby armadillo. Then he heard Crow breathing hard beside him, and Crow kicked it. And it flew, and he heard something snap, and a dull thud, and air escaping all at once.

When they got back to the van Crow climbed in the back. Floors could see him in the rearview mirror just lying there with his feet crossed, one pointed boot laying on top of the other, looking up at the ceiling of the van. And Floors could see blood on the pointed toe of the right boot.

He knew Crow from the reservation at Williams Junction. They'd grown up together, attending the little school at San Bernardino. He always knew Crow was headed for trouble. When they were barely out of their teens he'd hit a barman with a big granite ashtray over in Flagstaff. The guy went down like he'd been shot. He'd gotten away with that one, but trouble followed him, and he did a stretch in Perryville for manslaughter; killed some guy in a fistfight in a casino parking lot. When Floors first visited, he asked him what happened. Crow said he didn't remember much about it.

While Crow was in the State Pen, Floors got his life together. He started as a floor layer with his dad, Joe Tupi. Floor's dad told him there was a streak that ran through Crow's family: Like crooked teeth, he said.

Crow needed Floors to drive him about. His license had been revoked. Every month or so he'd drive him to his dealer, wait outside, Crow would buy two kilos of grass. When he got home, he'd get out his set of copper scales, bag it up, and sell it in twenty-dollar deals. Mostly he sold to college kids who'd drive out and smoke for a time, talking out of the side of their mouths to Floors, like they were living, and Crow would look at them like he was capable of murder.

Floors turned the key and drove, eating up the miles. For some of the time Crow sat up front drumming his fingers on the dash, saying nothing. The rest of the time he lay in the back and slept.

They were still in the high desert when Floors spotted a red church sitting in a field of scrub. He slowed and wound down his window. Then he stopped. There was an old weather-beaten sign in fancy writing at the edge of the field and it said: *Everything is possible for him who believes.* Reading it spooked Floors. He wound up the window and drove, without stopping until it got dark.

Then he looked in the back and saw that Crow was still asleep. So he stopped the van and got out. He knew there were low mountains maybe twenty miles to the east, he couldn't see them in the dark, but he didn't need to see them to know they were there. He thought he might like a joint. Instead, he lit a cigarette and looked up at the blue-black sky. At first, he just saw the bright stars, but when his eyes adjusted, he saw just how many of them there were, and then he saw all the little ones in the background, millions of them. They seemed to be getting closer – the more he looked at them – and Floors felt real small, smaller and lonelier than he'd ever felt.

He got back in the van and drove right through the night, didn't stop until they were at a gas station somewhere in Curry County, just outside Texas. It was early morning and he was hungry. He woke Crow and they both went in. It was one of those little windblown units that always made Floors wonder how the hell they ever made any money. He held the door open for

Crow and a little bell jingled. When he let the door go it sprang closed.

An old guy was sitting behind the counter. Floors lifted some chocolate bars and chips, then he noticed a little keychain figure of Jesus, arm half-raised, holding his pale blue robes. It was the last one remaining on the stand. He stepped closer to get a better look. It had been on that stand so long, the desert sun beating on it, that the robes were faded, the black hair gone.

– It's a Plastic Jesus, said the old guy behind the counter.

Crow stood at the back of the store.

– Like a rabbit's foot, he said.

– Luck don't mean nothing compared to faith, son, said the old guy, looking to the back of the store.

– How much is it? asked Floors.

– Two ninety-nine.

– I'll take it.

Floors put it on the counter.

Then he said: Can I ask you something?

– Go right ahead.

– If I was headed to Austin and wanted to go back to Arizona, is there another route, like further north?

– You trying to avoid the Border Patrol?

Floors didn't say anything; he just stood there,

looking right back.

– Son... I was your age, I found Jesus. Turned my life around.

Floors continued to stand there, silent.

– If I was you, said the old guy. You get to Austin, head north to Tulsa.

– Thanks.

When they got back to the van Crow said he'd drive from here on in. He took the keys off Floors and held up the new keychain to the light.

– What the fuck? he said. He doesn't have any hair. His skin's yellow. Christ in chemo. And he kept saying it: Christ in chemo.

Laughing out loud at how funny he found the whole thing. Then he took some stuff out of the pockets of his jacket. Small stuff mostly; gum, air freshener, chocolate bars.

Floors said: You ever think maybe you're a kleptomaniac...

– Yeah, said Crow. But I'm taking something for it.

And he laughed. And he continued laughing as he drove, like he was already high.

Floors lay down in the back and slept immediately. And he fell into a dream. In the dream, he was at a school, waiting to pick up a child.

Then Crow woke him.

– We're nearly there, was all he said.

Crow drove through maybe fifteen sets of traffic lights, then he turned left into a neighborhood of white stucco houses with neat sprinklered lawns at the front. When he got close to the pick-up point, he slowed the van, sat all hunched forward looking at the numbers.

Then he said: This is it, stay here.

Floors moved over to the driver's seat while keeping an eye on the house. He sat waiting, maybe twenty minutes, rolling the Plastic Jesus between his thumb and forefinger. And he looked at the house next door. There was a kid's tricycle laying on its side in the middle of the empty driveway.

When Crow came back outside, he had a big black sports bag slung over his shoulder. Crow looked up the street one way and then the other; and he rubbed and pulled at his nose, and Floors knew right away that he was high.

– Let's go, said Crow.

– You okay?

– I will be.

Crow guided him out through all those traffic lights and onto the highway. Then he lay down in the back.

Floors drove all through the day without stopping,

while Crow lay in the back clutching his bag. He headed up toward Tulsa, just kept following the signs until he made his way through Oklahoma.

That night they hit some fog. It started off as wisps that caught in the headlights and then all of a sudden there was a bank of it and Floors couldn't see a thing. It was so bad he could hardly see the front of the van. He couldn't pull over because he didn't know what it was that he was pulling over into. He was completely spent. So he just stopped, turned off the engine, climbed in the back, and slept.

The next morning something woke Floors from a dreamless sleep. A big guy in uniform, with a big cowboy hat in one hand, was looking in the side window, his other hand cupped over his eyes. It was the sheriff.

Floors woke Crow.

The sun was rising, and the fog had lifted. Floors had parked the car on a two-lane swing bridge. The bridge ran for about two hundred yards over a ravine. The van was parked right in the middle of that bridge.

When they stepped out of the van Crow gave Floors a look that scared him.

The sheriff put his hat back on and stood back a couple of yards from the van.

– You boys any concealed weapons?

– No, sir.

– Step over to the side of the bridge, put both hands on the rail.

– I couldn't see in the fog, said Floors.

– Put your hands on the rail, keep your feet apart.

As they did so the sheriff reached in and pulled the keys out of the ignition of the van. When he saw the Plastic Jesus key-ring he said: You boys all believe in Jesus?

– Yes, sir, said Crow.

– Uh huh. Well, I find anything in that van I shouldn't, you're sure as hell gonna need him.

The sun was up now but the moon was still visible. Floors put his hands on the rail, looked down in the ravine below, the mist rising off the water, and he looked at Crow. Crow was stood there looking straight ahead saying: Fuck, just quiet enough so the sheriff couldn't hear, but Floors could hear him all right. And then he said: I can't do any more time.

– Who's the driver? asked the sheriff.

– Me, said Crow.

– Driver's license?

– It's in my bag in the van.

– Go get it. Get them both.

This was way beyond anything Floors had ever

seen or done. He wanted to tell the sheriff that Crow planned to shoot him, but he just couldn't, he felt like he was nailed to the bridge, that his mouth was sealed shut. The sheriff was standing with his feet apart and he had undone the clip of his holster. Floors watched it all unfold as if he wasn't a part of it.

Crow got out of the van and handed their drivers' licenses to the sheriff. He was more alive now than Floors had ever seen him. And the sheriff seemed to sense it. He told him to move back over to the rail.

Crow said: Yes, sir.

And Floors knew by the way he said it he had the snub-nose in his belt, under his shirt.

– You boys any oustandin' bench warrants?

– No, sir.

– Uh huh.

Floors watched the sheriff turn to walk to his patrol car and he saw Crow reach down for the .38. But as he did so another patrol car pulled up behind them from the other end of the bridge and braked suddenly. A deputy hopped out.

– You okay, sheriff?

– Keep an eye on them a minute.

– Sure thing.

Crow spat into the abyss. The sheriff radioed through their details, then walked back real slow, slapping their drivers' licenses against his thigh. He walked past them and took a look in the back of the van, but not a real good look.

– Where you comin' from?

– Tulsa.

– Where you headed?

– Williams Junction, Arizona.

– Uh huh, said the sheriff. Anything in the back you wanna tell me about before I take a look?

– No, sir.

He slid open the side door of the van and Floors looked at Crow. He looked ill. Floors thought his knees would buckle. He didn't see any way out of this now. Then he heard a voice speak on both the police car radios, but he couldn't hear what the voice was saying through the static. The sheriff walked back to his car, only much quicker this time. He reached inside for the car radio and said something into it. And that same voice came back through the static. The sheriff said he was on it. Floors heard an engine start. When he looked behind him the deputy had driven off.

The sheriff walked back to the van, placed their IDs on the driver's seat, and the keys on the dashboard.

– You boys want a piece of advice, he said. When you get to wherever you're goin', stay there.

Then he got in his patrol car and drove past them, without even looking.

When they both got back in the van Crow took the gun out of his belt and said: I guess we just got lucky. He got an urgent call, had to take it.

Floors lifted the keys off the dashboard, but he didn't put them in the ignition immediately, he rubbed the plastic key ring between his thumb and forefinger.

– I'm going straight, he said.

– Sure you are, said Crow.

Floors turned the key in the ignition, looked to the far end of the bridge, and drove toward it.

The killing chair

Before the sun is up, they lead him through the basement corridor. He wears only a robe, and beneath it, cotton trunks. The two guards close either side of him make him look very small. Behind him are the warden and a round-faced Baptist minister. In his mind he imagines he's walking to the ring. He'd always wanted to be a boxer. On his cell wall is his only piece of contraband. A poster of a boxing colossus: the great Joe Louis. In the poster Louis poses, in an orthodox stance, with the world heavyweight championship belt wrapped snugly around his white shorts.

He told the minister he'd once seen his idol in the flesh. It was the only thing he really talked about.

In those final weeks, the minister had tried to teach him to recite the Lord's Prayer. He could say: Our Father who art in Heaven, Hallowed be thy name... and the minister would finish the prayer, standing there beside him in the small cell.

When they reach the death chamber the guards take off his robe. He throws a flamboyant uppercut and mumbles. Both guards place a firm hand on each shoulder, forcing him to sit. They strap his wrists and feet to the chair. He shivers as a tall, thin man in a black suit tapes a stethoscope to his chest. This same man then places a dish of small, white cyanide pellets underneath the chair.

He looks through the hard glass window.

A couple dozen newspapermen and witnesses watch and listen. One of the newspapermen – who's forgotten to remove his hat – says to his colleague: Only his God can stop it now.

After the men withdraw from the chamber, the tall man in the black suit waits exactly sixty seconds then pulls a string. Cold sulfuric acid pours onto the small white pellets. He holds his breath as the whitish-gray smoke rises slowly from the bowl. A large rectangular microphone has been placed in front of him; the type he has seen in dance halls. He clenches his right fist, pulls against the leather strap and says something. When he talks he must inhale. The white vapor escapes from his nostrils as if he is smoking a cigar, but he keeps talking – repeating the same thing over and over.

The man in the dark suit looks at his stopwatch: almost three minutes and he's still talking, still saying something. It should've worked by now; a day earlier it had worked just fine with a couple of dogs. But that was in the heat of the afternoon; now, in the cold early morning the reaction is cruelly slow.

He continues repeating the same thing over and over. The Baptist minister knows it's the opening lines of The Lord's Prayer, but the newspapermen can't hear, and he knows they need to hear.

The minister looks at them and whispers something into the warden's ear.

The warden nods.

Someone adjusts a dial.

Every single soul gathered hears clearly what he's saying.

– Save me, Joe Louis! Save me, Joe Louis! Save me...

Love is...

D octor Henry helped me get my new flat. While filling out my application form, he asked: Do you know what points mean?

I said: No.

And he said: Prizes. Points mean prizes.

Yesterday, when the trust bus dropped me off, I brought with me a single suitcase and a wipeboard. On the wipeboard I've written Lustral x 3, Olanzapine x 2, and below that, tea bags and Flora.

Whoever was here before me left everything; there's a TV, sofa, fridge freezer, washing machine, and a single bed. But there's one thing that bothers me. In the bathroom, above the sink, is a white rectangle in the surrounding blue of the wall where the bathroom mirror should be.

I'm lying on the sofa wondering why someone would take only the bathroom mirror when there's a knock on the door.

It's a girl. She's small with dark brown hair in a bob, and she has big brown eyes. She tells me her name is

Debs, and she says something about her brother and a letter. Sometimes, when I get an overload of information, I get a taste of copper in my mouth and I see snow falling.

When I come around, I'm sitting at the kitchen table. I blink and continue to blink.

– Are you okay? You look a little out of it.

– I'm fine. Thank you.

She tells me her brother lived in the flat before me. Her brother died, that's what she's saying. She talked to him on the phone that day. Later, she called to the flat and found him dead. He was a diabetic who fell asleep and didn't wake up again. She's waiting for his death certificate. It was posted to my address. She says she would have given everything she had to save him. I wonder how much that is.

– I left everything as it was. You're welcome to it. He would have liked that.

– Thank you.

– His name is... she stops and puts her hand to her mouth, was, Greg Warner.

I know that name. It's the name on the mail I put in the cupboard above the kettle. I reach up, open the cupboard door, and hand her the mail. She takes it in both hands and reads, but I know from her face the letter she wants isn't amongst the pile.

She starts to cry. I don't know what to do, so I hug her. Her hair smells of coconut.

– They said they posted it yesterday.

Then she says she has to go.

Before leaving, she gives me her mobile number.

After she leaves, I lie down again on her brother's sofa. She's perfect in every way. However, one thing still bugs me. Why did she take the bathroom mirror?

That night I dream of Debs and mirrors; the ones at Funderland that make you look all funny.

The next morning the first thing I do is check the post, but the letter isn't there. So, I phone Debs. She answers on the third ring. I tell her no post has arrived, but I'll be looking into it.

Then I go to the bathroom to brush my teeth. I look up while brushing – there's no bathroom mirror.

I phone Doctor Henry and tell him all about it. He says not to worry and not to overanalyse things. Doctor Henry says there's probably a perfectly good explanation as to why she might have wanted the bathroom mirror. He says I should put my thoughts on an imaginary train and wave goodbye to them.

When I hang up I try doing this, but it just makes things worse. I picture a big long train like you see in old black-and-white Westerns. As it pulls out of the station, Debs is sitting upright in every carriage, looking out of the window, waving goodbye.

The next morning I walk up to the Citizens Advice Bureau and ask how long it takes for a death certificate to arrive. The man behind the desk asks me how long is a piece of string? And I say: That depends.

I go over the whole thing with Debs, her brother and the bathroom mirror. He says it's intriguing. He also says I should call in person to the City Council offices. He says I need to look them in the eye.

The next morning a brown envelope is sitting on the OH NO NOT YOU AGAIN! welcome mat. I pick it up, but it's my rental agreement from the Housing Executive.

I phone Debs to tell her the letter still hasn't arrived, but I'm prepared to go with her in person to the City Council Offices. I also tell her there's something I need to discuss with her urgently.

She says she'll be there in ten.

Fifteen minutes later she still hasn't arrived. I'm about to phone her when I hear a knock at the door. When I open the door it's Debs. I invite her in, and she sits forward on the sofa looking up at me with her elbows on her knees.

I know our whole future hangs on her answer, but I just go for it.

– Can I ask you a question?

– Fire away.

– How come you left everything but took the bathroom mirror?

– I didn't take the bathroom mirror. It was like that when Greg moved in. I suppose he just didn't get around to fitting one.

Broody

Following an argument with my wife I've booked myself into this hotel; I may stay longer, I've yet to decide.

At the swimming pool, as I sit on the recliner, a man takes little baby steps out of the changing area. He's no taller than me but he must weigh over three-hundred pounds, and all of his weight is in his belly. Also, he has some sort of a skin problem, nothing major, just a redness and a dryness around his knees and elbows and down his shins.

He's bald on top with hair at the sides, and I think to myself: He doesn't have a cap. But, when he gets in the water, he puts on his cap. It must have been rolled up in his hand. The cap is the same as mine; you can choose black or blue, he's chosen blue. One size fits all, it says on the inside of the cap.

He walks through the water to the far end of the pool and does some aerobics, right knee to left elbow, left knee to right elbow. There are two women in the pool. One of the women – who's doing a slow breaststroke in a red cap – nods and he nods back without breaking his rhythm. When he gets to the far end he turns immediately and continues. The other woman gives him a thumbs up. This woman, in a black cap, is stick thin. She wants to talk, but he's in the middle of something.

I need to get a closer look. I walk down the steps and into the pool and swim over beside him. He doesn't seem to notice me – there's a blue rope between us – I'm on one side of the rope and he's on the other.

He begins taking shallow breaths like he's about to go underwater, only he doesn't go underwater; he walks through the water toward the other end of the pool, pumping his arms, like he's power-walking. He walks back and forth from one end of the pool to the other dragging all that water behind him.

When he returns, I let him get about a quarter of the way up the pool – a quarter is fair – and then I kick off. It's quiet under the water. It's different. The light is different, and the sounds are different. The sun makes sudden patterns on the small blue tiles on the bottom of the pool. I can hear my heartbeat in my eardrums, and I feel calm. For the short time I'm underwater I don't think of anything.

I overtake him when he's just over halfway up the pool, and I look at him underwater as I pass. I look

down at that belly, and his belly button sticking out –
like with newborn babies – and I think about my wife.
She'll come to her senses, I'm sure she will.

The Vallon Man

The high-pitched tone sounds over an area the size of a dinner plate. Sergeant Francis Kane stops immediately and runs the Vallon metal detector over the same patch of dirt.

Corporal Hicks is six feet behind, cradling his assault rifle.

As Kane marks off the suspected IED with white powder he's ignored by civilians walking down the road: an old man in the long shirt and baggy trousers of a shalwar kameez, his spine bent impossibly forward as he moves slowly down the dirt road; two girls, old enough to wear burkas, hurrying along, overtaking the old man.

Kane gets down on his stomach and angles the point of his bayonet into the dirt until it touches metal.

– It's basically an improvised Claymore, he says.

– Call in Ordinance, says Hicks.

– I will, don't worry.

The temperature is already in the high forties and the humidity is stifling. A slight breeze brings with it the smell of woodsmoke and human excrement.

– What do you think of the new CO?

– He's a dick. Now call in Bomb Disposal.

– Okay, I've seen enough. Tell them it's a DFC... multiple pressure switches.

Hicks speaks into the mouthpiece of the short-range personal radio attached to his collar.

– Directional Fragmentation Charge... multiple pressure switches, over.

Lieutenant Phillip McGovan is the new commander of 5 Troop, Bravo Company. He receives the message five hundred yards away, safely ensconced behind the heavily armoured Mastiff.

– How many pressure switches, over? he asks.

– How many switches, Frank?

– Multiple.

– He wants an exact figure.

Kane walks over to Hicks and switches off his radio.

When they arrive back at the Forward Operating Base, Lieutenant McGovan says: Sergeant Kane, a word.

Kane follows the lieutenant to a room with faded desert maps on the walls stuck with coloured pins, and cases of bottled water for seats.

– What happened with the radio today, Sergeant?

– The radio?

– I asked for information. I didn't receive it.

– You know this is my third tour, says Kane.

– Yes.

– Then you know that's the way I do things.

– In future, as your commanding officer, I'll get what I ask for. That's the way I do things.

– Is that everything?

– No, it's not, says the lieutenant. I'd like the men, all of the men, to shave daily before ops.

– Is that everything? Kane asks, again.

– That's all.

When Kane gets back to his bunk Hicks is stripping his SA80.

– What'd he say?

– Wants us all to shave.

– Three weeks ago he's on Dartmoor throwing thunderflashes, says Hicks. Now he's a fucking expert.

Kane clambers onto the bunk above.

– Why do you do it Frank? asks Hicks.

– With the lieutenant?

– No, fuck him. The Vallon, why the Vallon?

In their three tours together, this is the first time Hicks has asked him why. He takes his time answering.

– At the start I did it for the rush... that's the truth... but then I realised I was good at it.

– So, it's nothing to do with ego then? says Hicks.

– Fuck you?

Hicks considers telling his sergeant – and friend – that the world doesn't revolve exclusively around him. He decides against it.

– This'll be my last tour, says Hicks, reassembling his assault rifle. I'm out after this one.

The next day, Lieutenant McGovan lies in the dirt beside Sergeant Kane, looking through binoculars, beyond the crater caused by yesterday's exploded IED. The Marines, on the previous tour, lost four men on this short stretch of road. It has never been made safe and has always been considered a no-go area.

On one side of the road is the compound wall of the village, on the other, an irrigation ditch. McGovan hands the powerful field glasses over to Kane.

– You sweep the road, with Hicks covering you. The men will move in behind you with ladders to clear the alleyways behind the compound walls.

Kane puts the glasses down and stares at the dirt.

– Send in tanks and bulldozers.

The lieutenant stands up and dusts down the front of his combats.

– We can handle it.

Kane stands and faces him.

– You think so... you've the compound wall on one side of the road and the irrigation ditch on the other.

They've cut murder holes in the wall and there'll be IEDs in front of those murder holes.

– Then it's your job to find those IEDs.

– Listen to me, says Kane. If I lose any of my men today, I'm holding you personally responsible.

– You want a transfer? asks the Lieutenant.

– And leave my men in your hands...

Lieutenant McGovan stands momentarily staring at the sergeant, with absolutely no idea how to handle this man. Then he walks over to brief the rest of the troop.

*

Out front, Kane moves slowly, hovering the Vallon just above the dry dirt.

Hicks is behind him.

– You okay?

– That fucking CO.

– Forget the CO. Put your war face on, says Hicks.

That fraction of a second before the blast, Kane knows. He has enough time to think there's something unusual about a patch of fresh plaster on the compound wall before he's blown sideways into the edge of the irrigation ditch. When he hits the ground, he's still conscious. His goggles have been blown off, his eyes are filled with grit and his hearing has gone. He blacks out before he has time to scream.

The blast blows Hicks off his feet too. He scrambles up, staggers in the direction of Kane, unable to hear the sniper fire that kicks up dust all around him. Two of the men sprint forward, grab Hicks, and haul him back to the Mastiff, his heels dragging.

The rest of the unit takes incoming fire from insurgents hiding in nearby buildings. It takes them forty minutes before they can get in to retrieve Sergeant Kane's body. It's only when they carry him back to the Mastiff that they realise he's still alive.

Hicks looks down at his friend; the cams are peppered with blood and the right boot is gone. He can see bone. He vomits alongside the vehicle.

– Fuck this country, he says.

The Chinook arrives and carries both men out. Hicks is treated for superficial wounds. Kane doesn't regain consciousness until he's on a flight back to England.

He loses the toes and part of his right foot, is stippled with small shrapnel wounds, and there are red pepper burns on one side of his face. The blast plate he wore below his body armour saved his balls.

Following surgery, the physios tell him to slow down to allow his body time and space to heal. He doesn't listen – pushing himself to the absolute limit, driven by a desire to get back on his feet.

His men visit when they're on leave. He tells them all the same thing: he'll be back before the tour's over.

No one believes him.

After three months the minor injuries are healed. Each member of his rehab team is dumbfounded by his motivation: he swims every morning after breakfast, works out every afternoon in the gym.

After numerous miniscule adjustments, Kane learns to walk in handmade orthopaedic shoes. Immediately, he orders field boots from the same craftsman.

The day the boots arrive, Hicks comes to visit.

– How's the patient?

– Ready.

– Ready for what?

– I'm coming back.

– Look, I know what you're thinking, but forget it. I wanted to put a bullet in him myself. He's learned from his mistake. That's all it was... a bad mistake.

– It was forty minutes before my men got to me. He left me for dead.

Hicks looks around the ward. Most of the men are amputees.

– When I get back, I'm gonna kill him.

– Give up on this one, Frank.

– Next time I see you, Corporal, it'll be over there.

Less than two weeks later Kane is woken from his regular nightmare by one of the nurses. In the dream he's flying – it's exhilarating but the landing hurts like hell – there's an urgent call from a Corporal Hicks. Does he want to take it?

Kane takes the phone.

– What's up?

– It's Lieutenant McGovan.

– What about him?

– He's dead.

There's a silence.

– Frank, you there?

– What happened?

– IED.

– Anyone else hurt?

– No, that's it.

There's another brief silence.

– I just thought you'd like to know.

– Thanks, Hicksy. Stay safe.

– Okay, mate. Goodbye.

For the next two days Sergeant Kane doesn't get out of bed. He doesn't take part in any physio. There are no morning swims or afternoon visits to the gym. He talks to no one.

It puts him right back, the death of that lieutenant.

New Tank Syndrome

In the rec room is a large fish tank, containing Malawi Cichlids. Two tiny fish, no bigger than grains of rice, are wary not to venture too far from the safety provided by the nooks and crannies of the volcanic rock. During the four years George has been on the ward, they are the only fry to have hatched.

While George studies the tank, Doctor Guffy pulls up a chair.

– George, says the doctor. What do you think about leaving us?

– I hadn't thought about it, says George.

Doctor Guffy pushes his tortoiseshell glasses high onto the bridge of his nose and looks down at the last couple of pages of a yellow folder resting on his knees.

– We have your meds as good as we'll get them. I'd say you're ready.

– Where will I go?

– You remember Lorna?

George nods.

– Well, Lorna has a flat at the Avoca Complex.

George looks back to the tank.

– You'll still have regular appointments with me, says Doctor Guffy. And a community psychiatric nurse will visit once a week to see how you're doing.

On Friday morning, George walks into Doctor Guffy's office and says he's ready. The doctor reaches over the desk and shakes his hand. He suggests George find himself a hobby. Without hesitation George says his hobby will be tropical fish.

The psychiatrist smiles, gets up, and walks George past the rec room to the staff room. At the bottom of a built-in cupboard is an old fish tank. Inside the glass tank are some plastic plants, and a fresh bag of gravel.

That afternoon, George lifts the tank and carries it outside and onto the trust bus. Doctor Guffy follows with a single suitcase and wishes him good luck.

When the yellow bus arrives at the Avoca Complex, Lorna is waiting at the big metal front door. Lorna weighs three hundred pounds. She always wears black; big loose black blouses and long black skirts and wrap around things and dark mascara and various colours of Doc Marten boots. Her hair is always – intentionally or otherwise – a mess. When she was younger she was into Siouxsie and the Banshees; she hasn't quite got over it.

– Sometimes I might not answer the door, says Lorna. Maybe I'm sleeping, or it's the drugs, or else it's just me. If it goes on for more than three days phone the cops.

Lorna's been sober eighteen weeks.

Now she's addicted to the prescription drugs that helped her stay sober: Diazepam for anxiety, Cymbalta for mood, Zimovane to sleep, and Amitriptyline. She isn't quite sure what the Amitriptyline is for; she just knows she has to take it.

George likes his flat: the place is clean and furnished. While sitting on the sofa he wonders where to put his tropical fish tank. He decides to place it on a Mexican pine coffee table in front of the sofa.

The tank needs cleaning. George puts on the marigolds, bleaches the stones, the ornamental plants, and filter, and thoroughly scrubs the tank.

Then, basin-by-basin, he fills it with tap water, adds the bag of clean gravel, plugs in the light and filter, and flicks the switch. It all works.

He lies on the sofa staring at the pristine tank, listening to the filter, mesmerised by the water that passes out the other side in a current of miniature air bubbles.

Already he can feel his heartbeat slowing, peace coming into his life.

The next day, it's three in the afternoon before he wakes.

After taking his medication from his meds box he calls to see Lorna. He asks if she can drive him to Pets at Home.

– What time? asks Lorna.

– Now, he says.

Lorna owns a little red Micra. When they take off it lists to the driver's side like some doomed vessel.

Pets at Home is huge. There are so many fish George doesn't know where to start. An assistant, a boy of about sixteen, asks if he can help. When George tells him he wants tropical fish, the boy asks if he has kept fish before. George proudly tells him, Yes. The boy says they are doing a deal on neon tetras – ten for the price of seven. George buys ten; he also buys two red tetras and an albino debauwi catfish.

When he returns to his flat, he cuts open the clear plastic bag containing the fish and carefully releases them into the tank. The little white catfish dives straight to the bottom.

That night George can't sleep.

He gets up early, puts on his dressing gown and sits on the sofa watching his fish. The little catfish is misshapen: it has a humped back, long whiskers and big pink eyes. It's in constant motion, sweeping along the pebbles on the bottom of the tank, over and around the ornamental plants and up the glass sides, its mouth open for possibility. Sometimes, it darts at great speed to the surface then races back down to the bottom. George watches the little white catfish for hours, captivated, then falls asleep: this is his routine for the next few days.

A week later, George gets up to find one of his neon tetras floating at the top of the tank. The two red tetras take turns nipping at the body, nudging it along the surface. He gets a soup spoon from the kitchen draining board, takes the hood off the tank and scoops up the dead Neon, carries it carefully in front of him, in the style of an egg-and-spoon race to the kitchen, opens the pedal bin with his foot and drops the dead fish into the bin.

The next morning there's another neon tetra floating at the top of the tank. George looks down into the water and sees that one of the red tetras is also dead amongst the plastic plants.

Immediately, he calls to Lorna's, rings her bell, and waits.

When she finally opens the door, her hair is especially disheveled.

– Three of my fish died, says George.

– Three, holy fuck!

Lorna drives him back to Pets at Home.

The assistant, the boy who sold him the fish, says: It could be any number of things. Sounds to me like you might have a fighter.

– How'll I know which one it is? asks George.

– He'll be the last one left.

George looks at Lorna. Lorna looks at George.

Then the boy asks: What type of filter do you have?

– Just a normal sponge filter... it's old but it works... I cleaned it.

– You cleaned it?

– Yes, with bleach.

– Not good, says the boy. You killed all the good bacteria.

George stares at the boy.

– The bacteria in the filter break down the fish waste, cleaning the water.

– I didn't know that, says George.

The boy looks down at the floor, places one arm across his stomach, the other hand framing his chin, like an adult might do.

– It could be New Tank Syndrome.

– New Tank Syndrome?

– You need to give a filter time to build up the good bacteria that break down fish waste.

George looks at Lorna.

– Do you have the dead fish with you?

– With me... you mean like for an autopsy?

– Ah, no, says the boy. We'll replace the dead fish, but we need to see the bodies.

– They're in the bin.

– If any more die, just keep them in a bag in the freezer. We'll replace them then you can start over again when the filter's ready.

When they get back to the car Lorna says: It's a fucking KwikFit for fish. They don't fix anything, just replace it.

Each day another fish dies. Some days two are floating on the surface or sticking to the plants. The noise of the filter no longer calms George. Everywhere he goes he can hear it.

He doesn't answer his door for three days.

On the afternoon of the third day, Lorna phones the community psychiatric nurse who, in turn, phones Doctor Guffy. Doctor Guffy phones the police.

When they break down the door, George is asleep on the sofa beside the fish tank. They can't wake him. A blue medication box sits on the coffee table. It's Thursday but both Tuesday and Wednesday's pills are still in their respective compartments.

A single white fish floats on the surface of the tank, pushed along by the current of the filter.

Two weeks later, Lorna visits the mental health unit.

George has a chair drawn up in front of the tropical fish tank. As she approaches, he smiles a slow smile of recognition.

The two baby fish have grown a little, but they are still wary of venturing too far from the safety of the volcanic rock.

The butcher bird

The bus turned in a small dead-end circle of dust and drove past him the way it had come in, back up the main street of the village. It wasn't even a village really, just a collection of houses, a single hotel and a store.

Stanford watched the bus disappear in the heat haze and dust, unsure how he'd got there, where he'd even started his journey. He walked across the dry dirt road to the hotel. There was no one at the reception desk. He considered shouting; instead he walked on into the bar. A man stood behind the bar counter polishing a glass. He was the only one there. Stanford asked for water.

– Water, yes, said the barman. Large?

Stanford nodded, took out a stool, sat on it and dropped his Bergen at his feet. The man set the large chilled plastic bottle on the counter, unscrewed the lid and placed the glass he had been polishing beside it. Stanford lifted the bottle and drank greedily from it.

– You need a room?

Stanford nodded.

– We have rooms, said the man. I will need your passport.

– And a drink, said Stanford.

The man moved sideways, proud of the varied collection of bottles on the shelf behind him. Stanford saw a bottle of Old Grand-Dad Whiskey.

– Bourbon.

The man lifted the bottle from behind him and poured freely into a fresh glass.

Stanford drank the bourbon, draining the glass, and ordered another.

– How much for a room? he asked. Without a passport.

– For how long?

– For one week? said Stanford.

– In lira, euros or dollars?

He took off his money belt, unzipped it and looked inside.

– Euros.

The man paused.

– In euros, it is one hundred.

Stanford placed two fifties on the counter.

The man placed them in his trouser pocket.

– And for the drink?

– The drink is a compliment.

Stanford smiled.

– Thank you, he said. Can you show me to my room?

The man led him up to the first floor and into a small room with white walls and a single bed.

– If you need a fan it is an extra two euros per week.

– I'll need a fan, said Stanford.

Before the man closed the door, he said: Breakfast is between seven-thirty and nine o'clock.

Stanford placed his rucksack on the bed, walked into the bathroom and turned on the shower. It rattled before discharging a brown fluid. He let it run clear then stood in his shorts and vest with the palms of his hands on the tiled wall, his head bowed, watching the water slowly run clear as the dirt and dust washed from his hair and body, and clothes.

The next day Stanford awoke from the same dream that had been haunting him for months. As soon as he opened his eyes, he knew he was going to throw up. He made it to the bathroom and wretched so hard and for so long his stomach muscles ached. He lay on the cold, tiled bathroom floor and thought about the dream – the smell of cordite and burning flesh, his men unrecognisable.

He got up and placed his head under the cold tap for as long as he could stand it.

It was hot in the bedroom. The fan beside his bed was on at the low setting. The man must have come into the room after he was asleep.

Immediately, he looked for his money belt. It was safe and untouched.

From experience he had learned to travel light. He remembered his first patrol, how he had carried thirty pounds more than he needed, then the exhaustion, and skin rubbed raw from the webbing and his Bergen.

He dressed quickly in fresh shorts and a T-shirt and walked downstairs to the bar.

The man who had shown him to his room was watching football on the television.

– My name is Unal.

They shook hands.

– You missed breakfast, said Unal. You must be hungry.

Stanford couldn't remember when he'd last eaten. He ordered scrambled eggs.

– And to drink? asked Unal.

– Tea.

Outside, on the patio there was bougainvillea flowering. He took a seat at the only table, shielding his eyes. He must have lost his sunglasses; he would need to buy a pair.

Unal arrived with the scrambled eggs and tea.

Stanford ate as much as he could, pushing the scrambled eggs around the plate, but he had no real appetite.

When Unal came back to the table he asked: You were not so hungry?

– I thought I was.

Unal lifted the plate and carried it back to the kitchen.

During the next week Stanford got up each morning for breakfast of fresh bread, ripe beef tomato and feta cheese. Then yomped at speed until he was completely spent. In the early afternoons he slept with the fan on full setting. Then he came downstairs to pass the evenings in the company of Unal.

On one of those afternoons he washed his shorts and vest then hung the wet clothes over the warm balcony wall. The balcony overlooked a back yard and a lime tree. The ripe limes hung heavily from the branches and lay scattered in the red soil at the base of the tree. He wanted to pick one of those limes, although he had no idea what he would do with it once he had picked it.

A small bird, not much bigger than a sparrow,

lighted on a branch with a live lizard hanging from its mouth. The bird looked around cautiously, before impaling the lizard on a thorn. Stanford hadn't noticed the thorns, only the limes. When his eyes focused, he saw the bodies of lizards – four in total – impaled on the thorns. And he noticed that two of the lizards were still alive.

Stanford leant on the balcony and closed his eyes. Then he walked downstairs to the bar.

Unal saw the expression on his friend's face.

– I may join you? he asked.

– Of course, said Stanford.

Unal set two glasses on the counter, and poured two large measures, before adding ice and coke. Then he drained his glass and refilled it.

Stanford did the same.

Unal said: You shout out in your sleep.

Stanford wondered what it was that he was shouting out.

They drank in silence, then Unal asked: What is war like?

Stanford thought about this.

– You have a family, Unal?

– Yes, said Unal. I have a family.

– Imagine being unable to protect your family, said Stanford. That's what war is like.

Unal lifted the bottle and refilled Stanford's glass before filling his own. The two men drank into the evening. And then continued drinking.

Solidarity

It's mid-January.

On a secluded beach, two men sit on green fold-up fishing chairs, half-finished bottles of Bushmills at their feet, long barrelled shotguns across their laps.

Barney Hughes, a Catholic, joined the Royal Ulster Constabulary back in the eighties, when the paramilitaries were shooting Catholics just for being Catholic. It was the old RUC back then, now it's the Police Service of Northern Ireland, abbreviated to PSNI. Barney served in the force for thirty years as a constable, before taking the redundancy package with fringe benefits, that the perfectly accurate psychiatrist's report accorded him.

Billy Dobbin, a Protestant, joined the new PSNI to work with police dogs after taking a university degree in zoology. For the past ten years he's worked with cadaver dogs. His job is to find dead bodies. Now he's on sick leave, receiving Cognitive Behavioural Therapy, abbreviated to CBT.

Barney is currently five-three up in the seagull-shooting contest.

Untouchable

L ater that day, Mangus sat in the dirt at the front of the house sipping arak in the shade. The owner of the house, a respected Brahmin, allowed him to sleep at the top of the stairwell, as one might keep a dog.

He believed that Mangus, a native of the Irula tribe, practised black magic and would keep the house safe at night. The only thing he asked was that he swept the outside stone steps at the end of each week. In the two months Mangus had slept in that upstairs porch, he had only lifted the broom once, and the indignity off sweeping those steps set off such a drinking spree that he hadn't lifted the broom since.

Like all the people of his tribe, he was small in stature, dark-skinned, and a Dalit. Since he was a boy, he had displayed the skills for which his people are known: working the marketplace with his spectacled cobra, until the government banned such practices. Now he earned his living – such as it was – removing snakes from people's houses or businesses.

The sun wasn't yet at its height when a motorbike rider braked in the dirt and dust in front of him. The rider told him he must remain where he was: Doctor Dhoni, the Forest Reserve Manager, required his services immediately. It wasn't possible for the rider to take him on the back of the motorbike: he was an untouchable.

Mangus got up slowly and raised the bottle of arak to his mouth, finishing it. Then he told the rider that he had better go get his boss. As the motorbike rider spun off, he spat after it.

When the rider had disappeared, he walked up to the porch and placed a fresh bottle of arak into a large hessian sack.

Within minutes an all-terrain jeep arrived.

Doctor Dhoni, a big round man, leaned an elbow out of the window of the vehicle, looking closely to see if the little snake catcher was fit for the job. He did not care for this drunken Dalit. He observed that, although he was dressed in rags, he wore brand new Beni Badsha jute sandals.

When Mangus climbed into the passenger seat there was a smell of both fresh and stale arak. Dhoni made no comment. He simply wound down every window.

While driving, he told him what he knew. On the

very edge of the reserve, a boy had been bitten in the face by a large snake and died quickly. The description fitted that of a king cobra.

– When you see a king cobra, said Mangus, you will know it is the most intelligent of all snakes.

Without replying Doctor Dhoni considered this as he drove.

Within minutes, Mangus was asleep.

Doctor Dhoni reached forward, opened the glove box and took out a long thin bottle of budget aftershave.

While driving, he squirted it in the direction of the sleeping Dalit, emptying half the bottle.

It was a three-hour journey along dirt roads and, at times, places where there were no roads at all.

Mangus did not wake once, despite his head rolling from side to side as the jeep traversed the bumpiest of the terrain.

Doctor Dhoni knew they were approaching the village when he saw the circling crows.

It was typical of the villages that encroached the reserve: a cluster of simple houses with mud-plastered walls set among stretches of green fields.

Both parents had heard the noise of the approaching vehicle; they stood together at the entrance to their home: a small two-roomed hut of mud and cow dung with a sloped palm leaf roof.

The parents invited the Reserve Manager inside. It was not possible for Mangus, a Dalit, to enter the dwelling; he sat outside near the entrance on the hessian sack: his back resting against the mud wall of the hut, drinking from a fresh bottle of arak.

Doctor Dhoni was led to a wooden stool at a wooden table on a clean-swept, hard-dirt floor. The mother served three bean pancakes.

While he ate, both parents stood – neither of them touched the food – in accordance with Hindu custom while mourning.

Following the pancakes, the mother served sweet tea and a wooden bowl of boiled jaggery sweets.

Then she did something unusual; she carried a cup of hot sugary tea and the bowl of jaggery out-side to Mangus, placing both beside his sandals.

Doctor Dhoni lifted his head. He hadn't finished with the sweets. He thought he should say some-thing. He opened his mouth to speak but he didn't really know what it was he wanted to say.

From his seat outside, Mangus could hear the conversation inside the dwelling.

Both parents were inconsolable, they believed they had been cursed: the boy was their only child. They had called for a healer, but within an hour their son was dead.

Doctor Dhoni wondered when he would next eat. He asked where the healer was now.

The parents said he had vanished with the smoke of the cremation.

– We'll need to go into the plantation before it gets dark, said Doctor Dhoni.

He wiped his hands on his trousers.

– I will need you to take me to where it happened.

Both parents looked at each other.

– We cannot take you there. We can show you.

As they left the dwelling, Mangus peered inside. There were three stools sitting under the single table.

At the very edge of the ripe plantation, the parents held each other and pointed into the stout-jointed green stalks.

Mangus took off his new Beni Badsha jute sandals and placed them neatly on the red soil in front of the cane. Then he pushed aside the fibrous green stalks, and in a stoop, moved barefoot into the plantation carrying the hessian sack.

Doctor Dhoni placed a large laced boot into the cane, and reluctantly followed. The ripe cane grew well over both men's heads.

At a banyan tree they stopped.

Doctor Dhoni placed both hands on the tree's

sturdy trunk and stood, head down, breathing heavily. His brown shirt was stuck to him.

– They're tree climbers, said Mangus. Be careful.

Doctor Dhoni looked up into the foliage of the tree, then down at his boots. The black hairs on his arms bristled; he rubbed the back of his neck as if to remove something.

Mangus continued to walk further into the cane, smiling.

At a small clearing he stopped suddenly.

Doctor Dhoni almost fell over the top of him.

In the clearing, where the angled sunlight warmed the red soil, Mangus reached down and picked up a pair of children's sandals. They were small, but intricately designed, with bamboo leaf for the toe, and little amber beads sewn into the bamboo leaf for decoration. When he was a child, Mangus had worn a similar pair of sandals, made by his mother.

Both of the men then heard a low growl – it wasn't a hiss – it sounded more like a dog. Doctor Dhoni instantly backed away, falling over a nest of bamboo leaves. To their left, a king cobra had risen up to a full five feet off the ground.

The Reserve Manager had never seen anything like it; he estimated its full length at over sixteen feet. He had always imagined a silent killer; this creature had as great a presence as any large mammal.

In the clear sunlight, Mangus moved in front of the snake.

– Stay behind me, he said.

Doctor Dhoni obliged.

The snake moved her hood back and forward, measuring the distance between her and the man.

– We're between her and her nest.

Mangus moved and swayed.

The snake moved and swayed.

– You're warm from the sun, he said. I must tire you out.

The snake edged closer. And she struck down, fast, almost catching him.

– You killed a boy, he said. I know you didn't want to kill him.

He raised both hands, making small circular motions.

Doctor Dhoni was captivated by the open nostrils, the large scales on her head, the leaning hood, and her large bronze eyes were that of a calculating, intelligent creature. He hadn't expected that of any snake.

Mangus kept up a constant dialogue, talking now in his native tongue.

Sometimes the cobra would make fake lunges with

her mouth open, at other times she struck down, mouth closed, in what resembled a slap.

The Reserve Manager wanted to run, but he was drawn to the dance of death he was witnessing. Every movement was planned; this snake was thinking. Then he began to notice a change. She was more defensive now, less inclined to waste energy on strikes.

Mangus changed tactics too: moving his left hand in slow circles, keeping his right hand at waist height, in front of his body.

The snake continued to move her hood back and forward in front of the circling left hand.

Then Mangus reached up with his right hand and stroked the back of her hood, as one might pet a dog.

The cobra lowered her head towards him as he stroked her. The action appeared almost sensual.

At once, he had her head and mouth gripped. And he kissed the back of her hood, before placing the full length of her in the hessian sack.

Doctor Dhoni felt drunk with relief. He patted the snake catcher on the head.

– There's probably a male patrolling the area, said Mangus.

Doctor Dhoni involuntarily lifted his hands, looked down at his boots.

The two men made their way out of the ripe cane

and into the clearing. As they stepped out into the sunlight, they looked an odd couple: the sweating, rotund Reserve Manager and the diminutive dark-skinned Dalit.

Mangus set the large moving sack on the ground, before placing his feet carefully into his brand new Beni Badsha sandals. But he stopped momentarily, and looked back into the cane, before removing his feet again from the sandals.

– Where the bloody hell are you going now?

Mangus didn't answer; he simply disappeared back into the dark stalks of ripe cane.

Doctor Dhoni stood staring wide-eyed at the moving sack, his hands gripped under his chin.

Minutes later Mangus returned with the child's sandals. He patted the red clay from the soles, before handing them to the Reserve Manager.

– Give these to the mother, he said. It will help her.

The movement
of the earth

I moved away after I got out, I had no contact with anyone; the only woman I spoke to was the girl who worked the evening shift at the 7-Eleven.

I got myself a dog from the pound, a pit bull. His name was Jake, he had a history they said.

Jake knew it was going to happen a full minute before it happened. He sat on his haunches looking at me, his ears half-raised, the way they are when a car pulls up across the street. Then he started growling, looking at me, looking around him, looking back at me.

When the rumbling started Jake barked. And he kept barking.

The shaking was violent – all-powerful. The floor was moving. The whole room was moving; things were falling. Jake tore up a mystery thriller, which had fallen from the bookshelf and onto the floor. He was overexcited. I tried to calm him, but he wouldn't stop barking. I trusted Jake but I kept my face away from his jaws.

And then it was over.

I walked outside. The street was full of people, in ones and twos, all standing outside their houses, some on the footpath, some on the middle of the road. No one said anything. Most of them were looking up, speechless. I hadn't met any of my neighbors and I'd been there a year.

The woman from across the street was standing outside her house, wearing just a bathrobe. The bathrobe was black and silk with big orange fish on it. I'd seen her put her empty bottles in the trash can. She walked directly across the street and offered me a cigarette. It was a menthol, but I took it anyway.

Jake sat behind the fly screen watching. Then he started barking.

– It's okay, Jake, I said.

– There'll probably be an aftershock, she said. I'd wait until it's over before going back inside.

– I've never experienced an earthquake before.

– That was a big one. The one in eighty-seven was bigger, she said. But that was a big one.

She drew on her cigarette.

– Before it happens, when you think back, there's pure silence. The air is very still.

I thought about that. She was right.

– I'm Imelda, she said.

– Imelda... Elliott, I said. A pleasure to meet you.

– Likewise.

Then came the aftershock. I held Imelda. Imelda held me. It was a rush. I had an image of the road opening up and both of us falling into the fault line, but it was over quicker than the first one.

– You'd better get inside and calm the dog, said Imelda.

– Yeah, I said. Yeah.

There's no place like home

When Eddie Doyle returned from Iraq he moved back in with his mother and young sister. His mother was proud of him; but she was worried that maybe he had changed.

For Remembrance Day, he returned to the army base at Ballykinler – met up with his old army buddies – hugged each of them; they were his brothers. But, as the day wore on, he realised he wasn't a part of the family anymore. He was a civilian now, they were soldiers. There was a distance.

After that, he would drive alone in his car along the Strangford coastline. Some parts of the road he preferred more than others. At the mudflats he would pull over to the side of the road, sit in the car and watch the white egrets stalk the river mouth. Their long white bodies, their detached movement, drew him. Something about them reminded him of where he had been.

The family doctor prescribed sleeping tablets. They worked at the start, but not now, though he still took them. In the mornings when he woke, it would take time for him to gather his thoughts, he wouldn't get up immediately. It was necessary to try and process some of what he'd dreamt. Sometimes he would sleep till after lunch.

His mother said he needed to see a special doctor. He told his mother he'd picked up a parasite – there was a truth in that.

He walked downstairs – he wasn't sure of the time – it didn't feel like afternoon.

His little sister, Rebecca, greeted him.

– Hey lazybones.

– Hey.

His sister was still at school, he was older than her by seven years; it may as well have been a lifetime.

– You woke me up last night, she said.

– I did.

– You were shouting out in your sleep.

He was momentarily lost, wondering what he had shouted out.

– You gonna come see me in the play? she asked.

– What play?

– I told you. *The Wizard of Oz*. I'm Dorothy.

– You told me, said Doyle, trying to get something

234

right in his head.

His mother carried two cups of coffee to the kitchen table.

– Becca, let me have a word with Edward, she said.

Doyle sat down. He was ready for the coffee.

When the child had left the room, his mother asked: How are you today, son?

– Good, he said, adding milk to his coffee. I'm good.

He watched the milk cloud the coffee, rising in swirls, and he was momentarily gone.

– What about work? his mother asked.

– What about it.

– Well, don't you think it's time you looked for something?

He stirred the milk into the coffee.

– I don't know what it is I want to do.

– What about signing up again?

– You want me to go back there...

– No, I don't want you to go back. I love you son. I'm worried about you. You've changed.

He stood up, knocking his chair backwards onto the floor.

– I've changed? The whole fucking world has changed...

His mother put her face in her hands and cried.

Later that evening, he sat in his car in the school carpark. Two years previous he had attended the same school. Right now he struggled to remember a single thing about it. He finished the bottle of vodka, then quietly walked inside and sat in the cool dark at the back of the hall.

The play was almost over. He watched his little sister on centre stage.

She clicked her heels together.

– There's no place like home, she said.

Three times she said it.

The lights went out for the final act.

When the lights came back on, he was gone for good.

With special thanks to:

Liam 'Lucky' Jordan, Frankie 'Ninetoes' McClure, Darren 'Dolly' Albrighton, Charlie Lord, Ed Havlin, Joan Bryans, Gary Arbuthnot, Paul Roland, Dominique Delight, Conor 'Beardsley' Loughran, Dawn Pragnell-Kane, David Rogers, David Gaffney, Stephen Looney, Glenn Patterson, Owen McCafferty, Tammy Moore, Darren 'Diddy' Adamson, Dee Crooks, Mary Coogan, Peter Malone, Trevor 'Cooler' Smith, Ian Sansom, George Smyth, John Tubman, Mark Dobbin, Ronan Loughran, Mooglas O'Mooglahan, Claire Keegan, Lemn Sissay, Gary Kane, Box Rooney, Marty Looney, Mark Lally, Moya Forsythe, Julie Halliday, Fran Brearton, Davy McGuire, Paul White, Colin McCann, Vicky Heath Silk, Dave Archer, Davy Frankel, Charles O'Neill, Donal 'Locky' Loughran, Davy McNaulty, Peter Lally, Edmund Nixon, Tommy 'Hector' McIlwaine, James Stephens, Neil Baxter, John Magee, Shane Redmond, Tom Jordan, Elizabeth Enfield, James Parker, Jim Mallon, Ricky Lemon, Mark Kane, Michael J Jordan, Kerry Lemon, Sean Breen, Johnny Forrester, Con O'Reilly, Paul 'Atchie' Atcheson, Simon Kane, Ciaran Boylan, Tex & Angela McGinn, Eddie Young, Paul 'Zac' McGuire, Carmen Wilgar, Vanessa Black, Sheila McWade, Anne Colville, Maureen McParland, Timmy, Thomas & Chris...

Kingston University Press has been publishing high-quality commercial and academic titles for over ten years. Our list has always reflected the diverse nature of the student and academic bodies at the university in ways that are designed to impact on debate, to hear new voices, to generate mutual understanding and to complement the values to which the university is committed.

Increasingly the books we publish are produced by students on the MA Publishing and BA Publishing courses, often working with partner organisations to bring projects to life. While keeping true to our original mission, and maintaining our wide-ranging backlist titles, our most recent publishing focuses on bringing to the fore voices that reflect and appeal to our community at the university as well as the wider reading community of readers and writers in the UK and beyond.

@KU_press

This book was edited, designed, typeset and produced by students on the MA Publishing course at Kingston University, London.

To find out more about our hands-on, professionally focused and flexible MA and BA programmes please visit:
www.kingston.ac.uk
www.kingstonpublishing.wordpress.com
@kingstonjourno